THE MARQUESS'S PAINTING

Philip Marquess of Waverley
Rosalyn Fairchild

THE MARQUESS' PAINTING

A REGENCY ROMANCE

BLUESTOCKING BOOK CLUB
BOOK 2

ROSE PEARSON

© Copyright 2025 by Rose Pearson - All rights reserved.

In no way is it legal to reproduce, duplicate, or transmit any part of this document by either electronic means or in printed format. Recording of this publication is strictly prohibited and any storage of this document is not allowed unless with written permission from the publisher. All rights reserved.

Respective author owns all copyrights not held by the publisher.

PROLOGUE

A sudden crash made Phillip jump, the glass of brandy almost slipping from his hands. Setting it down on the table, he spun around and made for the door just as quickly as he could.

Already, he knew what this was.

"Oh, Phillip!"

Catching his mother's hands, Phillip looked straight into her eyes, the candlelight sending flickering shadows across her features. "Where is he?"

"The study," the Marchioness answered, her eyes red-ringed but her face pale. "There is already a great mess on the hallway floor. What am I to say to the servants? There are already whispers all over the county because of your father, and now there are sure to be even more!"

Phillip pressed her hands and tried to keep himself calm, despising his father for the pain and suffering he caused others by his selfishness. "I will manage this. Why don't you retire to bed?" Another crash made him wince, but he did not raise his voice. "Have Hannah bring you something to calm your nerves so you can sleep."

As though she had known she would be needed, the maid made her way towards them both, though she was dressed in her night-things, given the hour and the fact they had already been dismissed. "I am here, my lord, my lady."

Knowing that his mother's maid would take good care of her mistress and grateful that she had come to make sure all was as well as might be, Phillip ushered his mother towards her. "Go with Hannah, Mother. I will take care of the rest."

Hannah, who had been the Marchioness' maid for some years, led her away, and Phillip, relieved that his mother had gone without a fuss, turned his attention to his father. Shame began to build a fire in his chest as he walked along the hallway, noticing the smashed vase, the upturned table, and the ruined painting lying in pieces on the floor. The Marquess of Waverley was becoming well known for not only his foolishness with his wealth but also his dark temper and, though Phillip prayed his mother never heard of them, his dark deeds in shadowy places. This was the gentleman he called father, *this* was the man he ought to respect? It did not seem possible for Phillip to be able to do such a thing, not when his father led with such a poor example.

When it comes my turn to carry the title, he determined, *I shall never behave in such a way.*

"Father?" Pushing open the study door carefully, Phillip was forced to duck as something struck the wall beside him, sending smithereens all about him. Something sliced at his cheek. Instinctively, he raised his hand to his face, and the cuff of his shirt came back smeared with blood.

An indistinct roar of some sort of speech came from the figure that was Phillip's father. The Marquess was staggering this way and then that, picking up various objects and either flinging them hard against the wall or, after a moment's thought, replacing them back into their position. He did not even seem to be aware of Phillip's presence as he muttered one thing after another, anger threading through each exclamation.

Phillip's stomach twisted sharply and he sucked in a breath, keeping the door ajar so that he might escape if he needed. Lord Waverley had been known, in his anger, to attack a servant who had come to be of assistance to him, and thus, Phillip knew to be careful. It was also the reason he had instructed the household staff to stay far from the Marquess when he was in such a temper. Though Phillip did not have the authority to make such statements, it had been immediately accepted by those in the house. Clearly they did not want to have anything to do with the master of the house when he behaved in such a way, and Phillip could not blame them for that.

"Father!" he said again, more loudly this time. "This must stop at once!"

He winced inwardly as he said this, hearing an authority in his voice that he knew he did not possess and, truth be told, a little afraid of what the reaction would be to it. All the same, he drew himself up as tall as he could and tried to fill as much of the space in the room as he could in an attempt to appear as strong as possible.

"Why are *you* here?" The slurring of his father's words told Phillip everything he needed to know about his present state. "Are you come to make sure I am not spending all of your inheritance?" A shuddering sigh and a slamming down of one fist on the study table followed these words, making Phillip start with the vehemence of it.

"I think it might be a good time to retire, Father," he said, as calmly as he could despite the tension in the air. "Do you not think that – "

"The trouble is, my son, I *am* spending your inheritance." Lord Waverley tilted his head, though one hand lay flat on the study table now for balance. "A good deal of it, in fact." A faint smile lifted the edges of his mouth though it soon turned ugly. "Some of it now lines Lord Richardson's pockets, however, though I am sure he is nothing but a cheat and a scoundrel!" Walking away from Phillip, the Marquess lurched towards the small table in the corner, picking up the decanter with both hands and managing, somehow, to pour a full glass of whisky.

Phillip did not know what he ought to do, hearing his father shout various wicked insinuations about Lord Richardson, glad that, at the very least, none of the servants could hear what was being said. The fewer rumors that were spread, the better.

"It is just as well I stopped on my return home," Lord Waverley said, swinging around and then staggering so badly, he ended up half falling, half slumping against the wall, though the glass of whisky in his hand remained secure. "I would have had nothing but displeasure otherwise."

At this, Phillip turned away from his father, his stomach roiling. This was no way for any gentleman of honor, and yet, his father appeared to have no qualms whatsoever. Why did he choose to behave with such impropriety? Did he care nothing for the rumors and the whispers which were being sent all through the county about him? Did he not even think of the shame that was being brought to the Marchioness, as well as to Phillip himself?

"I need another drink."

"I think you have had enough." Phillip, forcing himself to take charge of the situation, turned back around and made his way directly towards his father. "You should retire,

Father. The study and the hallway will need to be tidied before tomorrow morning."

"Pah!" Yanking back his hand before Phillip could take the glass from him, Lord Waverley attempted to push him back with the other hand, though there was no strength in the action. "You are ashamed of me, are you?"

"Yes." Phillip spoke directly, looking back at his father with steadiness. "I am mortified by your behavior. You bring shame not only to yourself but also to your title and to this estate. What is worse, you shame your wife, my *dear* mother, by treating her as though she is of no worth to you." Whether any of these words would mean anything to his father, whether he was even truly listening, Phillip could not tell for the Marquess' eyes began to close and he swayed heavily on the spot, the anger visibly fading from him and instead, replaced with weariness. His shoulders dropping, all hope going out of him, Phillip unwillingly put one arm around his father's shoulders, relieved when the glass fell from his hand. Yes, the whisky would be another mess to clean up but having the Marquess removed from this room and into his bedchamber was all that mattered at the present moment.

"I know I have spent a good deal of money," his father muttered, leaning into Phillip as he made his way carefully to the door, silently praying that the Marquess would be this docile all the way to his rooms. "I care not. Nothing matters any longer, save whatever enjoyment I can eke out for myself."

This made Phillip's heart drop low, his gaze going from one disaster to the next as they walked along the hallway. Over the last few years, the Marquess had been doing these things more and more, becoming more and more ill-conceived in his actions and, truth be told, becoming utterly selfish with it. Phillip had always known, even from boyhood, that his father had a penchant for gambling, but now, it was as much a part of him as breathing.

Phillip dreaded to think just how much of his father's fortune would be left when the time came for him to take on the title. Grimacing, he ducked his head a little and continued slowly, bearing as much of his father's weight as was required as they walked towards the staircase. Quite how Phillip was going to heft his father up the stairs towards his bedchamber, he did not know. The man was becoming a dead weight, his eyes now closed, his feet almost dragging along the floor.

"If I might, my lord?"

Relieved to see the butler moving out of the shadows towards him, Phillip nodded and, in only a few moments, the Marquess was being helped up the staircase with Phillip on one side and the butler on the other. It took a few more minutes, and to Phillip, it certainly felt like an age, but eventually, the Marquess was in his room. Much to Phillip's disgust, the moment his father was placed upon the bed, he fell back, his eyes closed and his body sprawled out across the covers.

This was no way for any gentleman to behave.

"I shall take care of the master, my lord." The butler, always loyal, dependable and, much to his credit, trustworthy, inclined his head. "If you would grant me that, my lord."

Casting a disgusted glance in his father's direction, Phillip made for the door. "Of course. I thank you."

Once out into the hallway, he leaned back against the wall, closed his eyes, and took in a long, steady breath in the hope of calming his furiously thudding heart. It was not only the exertion of taking his father up to his rooms that had caused it, but the upset and the anger at all his father had done. No matter what Phillip said, no matter how much the Marchioness pleaded, it seemed as though the Marquess was set upon doing all that he could to ruin himself, and the family name with it.

I shall have nothing good to my name, Phillip thought to himself, running one hand over his face and squeezing his eyes tighter closed. *No young lady shall even wish to be in my company, let alone consider courtship!* For a moment, a face flashed in his mind, the face of a beautiful young lady of whom he had always taken note, but Phillip pushed it away at the very next moment. He dared not let himself think of her, nor let himself imagine what such a future might be like. With the family's reputation already stained, Phillip knew he could not let himself hope. Not even for a single moment.

A sudden cry and the sound of running feet made Phillip's heart lurch. The door to his father's bedchamber was thrown open, and the butler rushed out, only to see Phillip. Grasping his arm, the man looked into his eyes, ashen-faced.

"The master!" he exclaimed, as fear caught the back of Phillip's throat. "I went to him to see if I might waken him even a little but he would not wake."

Phillip frowned. "His drunkenness has led to unconsciousness, that is all."

The butler shook his head, swallowing hard. "No, my lord," he whispered, his fingers boring into Phillip's arm. "He is dead."

1

"Rosalyn."

She looked up from her book. "Yes, Fairchild?"

Her brother came to stand in front of her, his brow a little furrowed. "I forgot to inform you before we left for London that Lord Waverley may well be in society this year."

Her heart leapt. "Truly?" Lord Waverley was as dear a friend as could be to them both, though the loss of his father had kept them from his company for many a month. "It will be wonderful to see him. My last letter to him was only a few weeks ago but I do not think I mentioned London. Does he know that we will be here also?" She winced. "I do worry about what society will say of him." She had not heard a good deal of late but there had been some whispers and rumors about the late Lord Waverley that had disappointed her. Evidently, the *ton* believed that there was now very little coin left for the new Marquess of Waverley and some suggested that he was of the same ilk as his father – something that Rosalyn knew for certain to be false!

"Indeed." Her brother cleared his throat. "Speaking of society, we must speak."

The way his voice dropped low made Rosalyn frown and she rose to her feet, fairly certain that she knew what this discussion was to be about. "Speak about what, Fairchild?"

A slight lift of his chin and a narrowing of his eyes told her he was quite determined to have his way, though she silently told him he would not. "It is about all of this reading and learning that you do, these supposed *pastimes* that make you nothing more than a bluestocking." An edge of steel came into his voice. "You know how I feel about it, Rosalyn. It is time for it all to come to an end."

Instantly upset, Rosalyn shook her head. "No."

"You must! You now *must* think a little more about what society expects and act accordingly! You cannot – "

"Why must you protest so, brother?" Rosalyn put both hands to her hips and narrowed her eyes. "There is nothing wrong with my *pastime*, as well you know."

"Yes, yes, I am aware that you say that but it is not usual for young ladies such as yourself to do nothing other than read all the time." Her brother Daniel, the Earl of Fairchild, rolled his eyes at her. "And it is *certainly* not the inclination of most young ladies to demand that society recognize them as a bluestocking!"

Rosalyn frowned, dropping her hands to her sides. "Demand? I certainly do not demand that society approves of me, brother. It is only that I do not hide it. You know as well as I that our late father very much approved of my learning."

With another sigh, her brother pushed himself up in his chair so he did not slouch as much as before. "He did, yes." His nose wrinkled. "And mother does as well, for she gave me a very severe talking to before I left for London, stating that I was not to discourage you in any way."

"And yet, here you are doing that very thing."

This made her brother grimace, one hand rubbing over his chin. Silence fell and Rosalyn chose to take a seat opposite him, holding his gaze steadily but refusing to let the conversation go. Ever since they had come to London some weeks ago, Lord Fairchild had been eagerly pursuing the young ladies of London and had seemed to forget about her.

Until this afternoon, it seemed.

"In truth, Rosalyn, it is this nonsense about being in a 'book club' that has concerned me." Shifting in his seat, he glanced at her but then looked away. "Whatever does that mean? And why must you publicize it in such a way?"

"Publicize it?" Hearing the tension in the way her voice rose, Rosalyn took a moment to collect herself so that she might speak calmly. "Fairchild, you must know that we are not *publicizing* it as such! It is only that we do not hide it from the *ton*, just as we do not hide ourselves from them either. Besides which, is it not as though we are going to have a good many other young ladies seeking us out, eager to join us, is it?" She managed a quiet laugh at this, thinking of what it would be like should hordes of young ladies begin to seek out herself and her friends, all in the hope of joining their bluestocking book club. "That is not something that will occur, I am quite sure of it."

"As am I." Lord Fairchild scowled but continued to look away from Rosalyn as though he was a little embarrassed to look into her eyes. "I do not wish you to be ridiculed, Rosalyn, that is all."

Searching her brother's face and being fully aware of the way he could not look into her eyes, Rosalyn let out a small sigh. "Daniel, I think that if you were to be honest with me –

and with yourself – you would admit that it is *yourself* that you worry about, is it not?"

He said nothing but cast his gaze down to the floor. Pain struck Rosalyn's heart but she continued on regardless.

"I can see that you are hoping to make an attachment yourself this Season," she said, speaking softly in the hope that it would show her brother her understanding. "Naturally, you want to make certain your reputation is pristine and that there is nothing to bring you any sort of shame."

Slowly, his gaze began to lift.

"But I am not something to be ashamed of," she finished. "My love of learning is not something you can hide, I am afraid, and I will not pretend to be anything other than that. Any young lady of quality, however, ought to be accepting and considerate, so I sincerely doubt you have anything much to trouble yourself with."

This made her brother shift in his chair, one hand rubbing over his mouth as he finally caught her gaze. He sighed heavily but then turned his eyes away from her again. "I do not think any young lady of quality ought to be engaged in as much learning as you are doing."

She shrugged, having heard such a sentiment before. There were no words accompanied by such an action, and this made Lord Fairchild sigh, though again, it made no impact upon Rosalyn in any way.

"You are not going to desist, are you?"

Shaking her head, Rosalyn spread out her hands. "I am not going to turn from this, brother. The sooner you come to understand that and accept it, the better it shall be for us both."

With a grimace tugging at his lips, he nodded and then pushed himself forward to the very edge of his chair, as though he were going to rise from it. He did not, however, finally looking long at her, as if assessing whether or not she would, in any way or any capacity, change her ways.

With a long and almost mournful sigh, it appeared to Rosalyn that he accepted she would not, and with another scowl, he finally rose to his feet.

"Very well. I shall do my utmost not to bring this subject to the fore again, though I confess that I am not at all pleased to hear about this 'Bluestocking Book Club' – and even more displeased that I had to hear about it from Lord Gillford rather than from my own sister!"

Rosalyn spread out her hands. "If I had told you of it, would you have shown any pleasure whatsoever? Would you have sought to garner understanding? Or would you have become frustrated and railed at me for some days about it all, seeking to put an end to it all?" She spoke gently but with enough firmness to make her brother's head drop. "And then, would you and I have argued a great deal? Would we not have become upset with one another and might have been greatly displeased with each other! I did not want that."

Her brother rubbed one hand over his eyes but, with a hiss of breath, dropped his hand back to his side and looked at her. "I suppose that you are right. I have always tried to dissuade you – without success, I might add – and I would have done the very same with this. I do wish that our late father had made you more of a lady, Rosalyn."

These last few words sent a dagger into Rosalyn's heart, and though she tried to open her mouth to respond, she could not. Tears began to form in her eyes, and she blinked furiously, desperate now to keep her composure until her brother took his leave of her.

It did not take long. With another clear and heavy sigh, Lord Fairchild quit the room, his final few words still doing all they could to shatter Rosalyn's heart. The moment the door closed, Rosalyn put her head in her hands, her elbows on her knees as she sat forward, her chest tight and her heart aching. To her mind, their late father had raised both her and her two brothers in a manner most fitting, for both of her brothers were well known in society as excellent men of good standing with fine character. She had been given the opportunity to learn just as much as she wished and had reveled in it, just as she did now, and though she had been given instruction about propriety, dancing, and deportment, she had also been taught about mathematics, history and even politics. Whatever it was she had desired to know, her father had encouraged her in that and her mother also! It was only her brother who had ever pushed away the suggestion that being a bluestocking was a great, terrible thing. To his mind, she was ruining her own reputation by having such a determination to learn.

Drying her tears, Rosalyn tried not to let her brother's sharp words push any further into her heart. She had friends here, she reminded herself, *good* friends who would do anything they could to assist her. They had already done some good with their 'Bluestocking Book Club', though their meetings had been a little less about the books they were reading and a little more about solving a mystery!

Though it came right in the end, Rosalyn thought to herself, sniffing lightly as she rose to her feet to ring the bell for tea, hearing a scratch come from the door at the same time. *Joceline is happy and I am truly delighted for her.*

As if her friend had known she was thinking of her, the footman came at that very moment with Miss Joceline Trentworth's calling card. Instructing the footman to bring tea for them both, Rosalyn waited with eager expectation for her friend to arrive, rushing forward to hug her the moment she stepped into the room.

"Oh, I am so very pleased to see you!" she exclaimed, her heart lifting in an instant, pulling away from all that her brother had said to her. "Should you like to take some tea?"

Her friend smiled. "Yes, I thank you. Though I cannot stay for too long, for there is dinner to prepare for. I am to join Lord Albury for dinner this evening, along with his other guests."

Rosalyn beamed at her. "How wonderful. You are courting now, yes?"

"Yes." With a soft smile, Miss Trentworth tipped her head just a little. "It was very difficult at some junctures, I confess it, but it has been worth walking through those difficulties to reach where we are now."

Rosalyn's smile lost some of its strength. "My brother has only added to my difficulties, unfortunately." As the maid brought in the tea tray and set things out, Rosalyn recounted all that had been said, including the final sentence, which had brought her such severe pain. Miss Trentworth listened carefully, though Rosalyn could tell from the shadows in her eyes that she was not in the least bit pleased by it all.

"That must have been very difficult to endure," her friend said, when Rosalyn had finished. "Though I must hope that you are not about to turn from us all?"

"Certainly not!" Rosalyn declared, her chin lifting. "I told him that I had every intention of continuing just as I have always done, that the bluestocking book club is not something I would turn from."

"That is good." With a brilliant smile, Miss Trentworth leaned forward in her chair. "For I had come to suggest that we might meet again very soon, mayhap this week, if it would please you?"

Rosalyn's heart lifted in an instant. "Yes, it would, very much indeed."

"Excellent." Miss Trentworth's expression gentled. "I do hope you know just how much help you provided to me and Lord Albury with the missing necklace, Rosalyn. We could not have found the truth without your diligent study."

This made Rosalyn smile, the wound inflicted by her brother slowly beginning to heal at the encouragement of her friend. "Thank you, Joceline."

"I mean every word," came the reply. "Though mayhap now, we will be able to settle into reading our books and discussing them at the book club, rather than discussing what we have learned about the necklace and its disappearance!"

This made Rosalyn chuckle as she picked up her tea. "I am quite sure that no matter what we do, I shall be contented," she said, with a smile. "Although I shall admit it would be wonderful to discuss what we have been reading! I have learned a good deal about one particular artist that I should be delighted to share with you all."

"And so you shall," came the determined reply. "The bluestocking book club will meet very soon, and you shall tell us all about this artist and all you know of him."

Rosalyn beamed at her friend, reaching for her tea and finding her heart entirely healed. She had her friends, she had their book club, and whether her brother approved or not, that was all that she needed to be happy.

2
———

Walking through London ought not to bring a gentleman out in a sweat, but Phillip's entire body was hot and clammy. It was the first time he had ventured out into London since his arrival some three days ago, but even now, it felt as though every eye was lingering upon him... and a fresh darkness coming into every expression as they realized who he was. Barely able to bear the looks and quite certain there were whispers pursuing him, Phillip quickened his steps, eager now to make his way to Whites as quickly as he could. There was no need to linger here, no need to stop, nod, smile and even converse with some of the other gentry. There was no promise of amiability with anyone that he *did* stop to speak with and thus, Phillip continued on his way with long strides and a head ducked low.

It had been a little over fifteen months since he had taken on the title. Casting his mind back to that fateful night when the butler had, horrified, rushed out to find him, Phillip shivered lightly. It had been a night unlike any other, a night when he had not only found himself broken by sorrow and grief but also battled the niggling sense of relief that had come with it. He had not told his mother of what had happened until the following day, wanting her to rest from the night's upset before he added to them. When he had done so, he had seen that same relief in his heart mirrored in her eyes.

They had never spoken of that emotion though Phillip knew, even now, it was there. He battled it still, hating himself for all he felt, and yet, at the same time, glad now that he could bring the title back into some sort of good standing. The mud that clung to it still, however, was significant, and Phillip knew it would take a good deal of time and effort before such a thing was possible.

Stepping into Whites, Phillip let out a slow breath as the door was closed behind him, feeling as though he were walking into a sanctuary. Here, he would be safe from the crowd and, whilst there would be some gentlemen unwilling to be in his company given the poor state of his family name, Phillip hoped he would find some friends here.

"A brandy." Speaking to one of the footmen, Phillip made his way further into Whites, selecting a chair in the corner where he might sit in solitude. If anyone wished to join him, they would be more than welcome but Phillip did not mind sitting alone. After the last eighteen months, his mind felt constantly weighted, he was plagued with heavy thoughts that took any sense of happiness or contentment from him. Perhaps here, he would be able to find even a little of that.

"Stepford? Is that you?"

Phillip turned his head, a little surprised to hear his old title on someone's lips. "Lord Mansfield?"

"The very same!" A gentleman he had not seen in some

two years shook Phillip's hand firmly. "Goodness, it has been much too long, has it not?"

"It has been many months since I have been in society, yes," Phillip admitted, as his friend came to sit down in a chair opposite. "Though I am not Lord Stepford any longer."

Lord Mansfield's face fell. "Your father?"

"He died some time ago," Phillip replied, aware that he felt not even the smallest hint of sorrow upon saying those words. "I have now taken on the title."

Lord Mansfield's eyebrows lifted. "So you are now the Marquess of Waverley."

Phillip nodded. "I am."

"My congratulations and my sympathies," came the reply. "I am truly sorry, I had not heard of his passing." His eyes flicked away from Phillip for a moment, a shade of red touching his cheeks, and instantly, Phillip's heart grew heavy.

"You *had* heard of some other things, mayhap," he said, with a grimace. "Do not be afraid to speak of such things to me, my friend. I am well aware of my father's poor reputation." The grimace grew into a scowl. "I just did not realize that it had come all this way to London."

"I am afraid his escapades have been spoken of in many a gathering," Lord Mansfield told him, somewhat bluntly. "I am sure that not everything that was said of him was the truth but – "

"You might find yourself surprised there," Phillip answered, grimly. "My father was not a good man, Mansfield. The last few years of his life, he became more and more repugnant in his behavior, to the point that I became utterly ashamed of him."

Lord Mansfield's lips flattened. "That must have been difficult for you to bear."

"It was more the pain that he caused my mother that troubled me," Phillip answered, quietly. "I am well aware that my family name has been quite ruined though I must, now that the mourning period is over, do what I can to improve it."

"And is that why you are in London?"

Phillip nodded, taking a sip of his brandy.

"What is it you intend to do?" his friend asked, gesturing to the footman to bring him a drink also. "Have you specific plans as to what you ought to do?"

This made a flush draw into Phillip's chest, spreading up to his cheeks. "Not as yet. But in truth, I could not linger at my estate any longer. My mother has been pale and wane for too long and I *had* to have her improve in some way."

"Then she is in London with you?"

"She is." Phillip bit his lip, then shook his head. "I think she will fare a good deal better than I, for her friends and acquaintances will know she had nothing whatsoever to do with my father's foolish behavior. Though I must confess, I hope that I have not done wrong by bringing her here. I hope she will not be rejected by the *ton*."

"I am certain she will not." The encouragement in Lord Mansfield's voice made Phillip smile. "Just as I am sure there will be many more than willing to have *you* in their company, my friend. There will be some unwilling but they need only be ignored for their foolish opinions. You need not fear rejection."

Phillip winced. "I hope not."

"And who is this you are speaking with, Mansfield?"

Putting a quick smile on his face, Phillip waited for Lord Mansfield to introduce him to the gentleman who had meandered over, noting that a second fellow was following the first. Lord Mansfield, however, did not smile and

The Marquess's Painting

certainly showed no willingness to continue the conversation, throwing the gentleman a glance and then rolling his eyes thereafter.

"Lord Hemmingway, good evening," Lord Mansfield grunted. "If you would excuse me, we are in the middle of a conversation, as you can see."

"And all I was asking is the name of this gentleman." The man that Phillip now knew to be Lord Hemmingway gestured to Phillip, though he did not much like the glint in the man's eye. "It is not often that I see you in the depths of conversation with only one other! Usually, you are at the heart of whatever is taking place, surrounded by both gentlemen and ladies!"

"I know your face." The second gentleman gestured to Phillip, though he did not recognize the fellow. "We must be acquainted already though I confess that your name is quite gone from my mind."

Phillip's smile grew fixed. Clearly, these two gentlemen brought nothing but trouble with them, and Lord Mansfield was doing his utmost to keep Phillip from that. "I do not think we are acquainted, actually," he said, as the first gentleman narrowed his eyes a little. "I have not been in London for some two years now, you understand."

The second gentleman opened his mouth and then closed it again, looking away.

"Waverley!"

A loud exclamation made Phillip sit up straight, the brandy sloshing gently in the glass. He could not see whomever had spoken his name and nor could he ascertain whether or not it was meant as a pleasant greeting or something else.

"I am delighted to find you here!" the voice said, just as someone elbowed his way in between the two as yet unintroduced fellows. "I received your letter and did not have time to write to you to say we would be in London also! How good it is to see you again."

Phillip got to his feet, a wide smile splitting his features as he shook Lord Fairchild's hand. At the very same time, the two gentlemen who had been irritating Lord Mansfield took a step back, though Phillip did not miss the way they glanced at each other. "I am very glad to be in your company again, my friend." He had not known that Lord Fairchild, one of his oldest and closest friends, would be in London also, though part of him had been hopeful he would be present. "And thank you for your letters. They have been a great encouragement to me these last few months."

"Of course." Lord Fairchild glanced around him, then frowned. "Is there a reason that you are standing here, Lord Hemmingway, Lord Pentland? I did not think you were acquainted with the Marquess of Waverley."

The two gentlemen exchanged another glance, though Lord Hemmingway smiled in a cold fashion that made some of Phillip's contentment fade.

"We were seeking an introduction, though now, of course, we need none whatsoever! Everyone knows who Lord Waverley is, I am sure."

Phillip frowned. "I think you mistake me for my father, gentlemen."

Lord Pentland snorted and shrugged his shoulders. "Mistaken or not, we know the reputation of your family. A throwing away of good fortune over foolish, nonsensical things? A penchant for seeking out ladies of the night in as many different places as they could be found? A dark temper, a mean disposition?"

"Tell me, Lord Waverley, do you have any coin left?" Lord Hemmingway asked, with a chuckle that made Phillip's anger flare. "I am surprised you have two coins to rub together, given all that your father threw away!"

"That is enough," Phillip answered, taking a step closer to the two gentlemen, with Lord Mansfield also getting to his feet to come to stand beside him. "You will soon find, as will the rest of the *ton*, that I am not my father."

Lord Hemmingway laughed. "I do not think it matters the sort of gentleman *you* are, Lord Waverley. The only thing that matters is what the *ton* think of you – and I can assure you, it will be very little."

"It will be more than we think of you!" Lord Mansfield exclaimed, as Lord Fairchild stepped forward in a manner that told Lord Pentland and Lord Hemmingway that they ought to say nothing more.

"Either take your leave or we shall accompany you to the door," Lord Fairchild gritted out, as Phillip's hands curled tightly. "There is no need for any of this."

Thankfully, Lord Pentland and Lord Hemmingway took a moment before turning away, their steps leading them towards the door. As Phillip watched, however, their heads came close together and one cast him a glance over his shoulder before returning to whisper about him again. His heart, however, did not flood with relief, as he had expected. Instead, he found himself worried about all that these two gentlemen had said, afraid that the *ton* would reject him utterly.

"You need not be concerned," Lord Fairchild said, as though he had read all that was in Phillip's thoughts. "You still have friends here in London."

Phillip nodded. "That is true enough, at least."

"Though there certainly will be those who do not wish to be in your company, that is certain," Lord Mansfield said, with a shrug. "We have spoken of that briefly already so I know that you are aware of it. As I have already said, you need not fear rejection, my friend."

"I thank you." Phillip caught the attention of the footman to signal for more drinks. "I do not much like what will be said of me, however. It is a great frustration to know that they consider *me* to be of the same ilk as my father, and all without having any knowledge of my character! What is there to be done about that?"

Lord Fairchild and Lord Mansfield exchanged a glance.

"Nothing," Lord Fairchild said, with a sorrowful smile. "I am afraid to say, my friend, that there is nothing you can do about that and thus, you must now only seek to prove *your* character in as many ways as you can. Though you will have us friends enough to help you do so." His expression brightened. "And I will make certain to bring Rosalyn to you, so that you will have someone to dance with! That will make the other young ladies of London take notice of you, I am sure."

At the mention of Rosalyn, Phillip's heart dropped, only to rise up again in a rush. He managed to smile and nod and thankfully, the footman brought over their drinks so the conversation did not need to continue... but Phillip's mind was centered solely on the lady his friend had mentioned.

Lady Rosalyn was the sister of Lord Fairchild and thus, Phillip knew her well enough given that he and Lord Fairchild had been such good friends. What he had never once mentioned to Lord Fairchild and certainly had never even *thought* to say to Lady Rosalyn was that his heart had always held a modicum of affection for her. It had not been anything severe, had never become anything of note but all the same, Phillip knew it was there.

But I will never be worthy of such a wonderful creature, he reminded himself. *Not after the reputation my family now holds, not after the loss of fortune my father left me with.* Closing his eyes for a moment, he took in a breath and then gave himself a slight shake. Seeing Lady Rosalyn again would be a very lovely thing indeed, he was sure. He simply did not need to even *think* about her in any other way other than friendship, for that was all he could ever offer her.

3

"I confess, I am a little disappointed!"

Rosalyn looked in surprise at Lady Amelia. "Oh? And why would that be?" They had only just concluded the meeting of the bluestocking book club, and Rosalyn had enjoyed every moment of it! It was a little surprising, if not disappointing, to hear her friend say such a thing.

"I am disappointed that we have no mystery to solve," Lady Amelia replied, with a twinkle in her eye as Rosalyn's shoulders dropped, her smile returning. "Though I did enjoy our conversation about all we have each been learning of late and indeed, of the new books we have been reading, there was a part of me hoping that we would have some great and mysterious event to discuss as well!"

This made the other ladies laugh, though Rosalyn too had to admit there was a part of her that felt the same. "I know how you feel, Amelia," she admitted. "I think we found such contentment with the affair of the necklace because it felt as though, for the first time, our skills and our knowledge were being taken seriously *and* that we could use them for the good of someone else." She lifted her shoulders and shrugged, sighing heavily. "Most of the time, we are left to feel as though everything we are doing is quite wrong and ought to be stopped in an instant!"

"Yes, I feel that too," Lady Isobella agreed, her lips in a rueful smile. "We are so often pushed away, are we not? And yet, when it mattered, all that we have learned and all that we have within ourselves was of use!"

"Mayhap I can have Lord Albury lose his heirloom again," Miss Trentworth said with a smile, making every other young lady laugh. "Though, mayhap, it will come to us soon enough."

Rosalyn smiled, nodded and made to say something, only for the door to swing open and, much to her surprise, her brother strode into the room with another beside him. He stopped short upon seeing them all gathered there and Rosalyn, lifting an eyebrow, tilted her head a fraction, silently asking him what he was doing striding into the room as he had done. Had she not told him over breakfast that her friends would be coming to call later that day? Had he truly been so very distracted that he had not listened to a word coming out of her mouth?

"R – Rosalyn." Lord Fairchild blinked quickly, his gaze on every other face before finally returning to her. "I did not realize that you had company."

Rosalyn lifted her eyebrows. "Is that so, brother? I am certain I spoke to you about it all over breakfast this morning." Her gaze went to the gentleman beside her brother only for her heart to lift with a sudden delight. "Though now that I see who you have brought with you, I cannot hold any sort of frustration against you!"

"We shall all take our leave." Miss Sherwood came towards Rosalyn and smiled, just as the other ladies gathered their things. "We have finished our meeting already, have we not?"

"Yes, we have." Rosalyn smiled at her friend, then looked to the others. "Though are you not all attending Almacks this evening? I will see you all then."

With nods and murmurs of assent, the ladies left the room, with Lord Fairchild bowing to each one before they quit the room. The moment the door closed, Rosalyn moved quickly to greet Lord Waverley, a bright smile on her face and happiness bubbling in her heart.

"Rosalyn." Lord Waverley made to bow but Rosalyn, holding nothing back, embraced him quickly. His arms went around her and Rosalyn held him tightly, feeling him just as much family as her brother was.

"Oh, Waverley, I am so very sorry for the loss of your father." Stepping back, she caught his hands and looked up at him. "That must have been very painful indeed."

He smiled sadly, his green eyes searching her face, his brown hair swept lightly to one side of his forehead. "It has been, though I am sure you have heard all the whispers and rumors about him, yes?"

Rosalyn said nothing, seeing the pain in his eyes.

"But I am come to London nonetheless," he continued, when she remained silent. "I could not let my mother continue to reside at the estate any longer, for she has been melancholy for a long time and I do not want to see her so."

"And she has found some friends here?" Rosalyn asked, pressing his hands and then releasing them. "You both have, I hope?" She did not mention that she had heard everything that there had been to say about the late Marquess of Waverley, for some of the rumors had been very dark indeed – and part of her had not wanted to believe them to be true. At the same time, she knew very well that he would find it a little difficult to find many friends here in London, for there were many whispering about his father's antics, with many wondering just how much of a fortune Lord Waverley still had.

"I have found enough to keep me contented," Lord Waverley answered, though the smile was a little tight. "It is a great frustration to me that so many of the *ton* will not listen to what I have to say nor judge me on my own character! Instead, they are determined to think what they please about me, based solely on the sort of character my father had." A heaviness settled into his expression, his eyes going to the floor, his shoulders dropping. "You should, I think, be careful of being seen in my company in public, Rosalyn. I am sure it will do you no good whatsoever."

"Nonsense." With a wave of her hand, Rosalyn disregarded his warning and then gestured for him to sit down, with her brother going to ring the bell for them all. "As my brother will tell you, the opinions of the *ton* mean very little to me. Much to his displeasure, I might add!"

"Oh?" Lord Waverley settled down into a chair, though his eyes went from Rosalyn to her brother and back again. He did not ask any specific questions, did not ask what it was that she meant by that, and yet Rosalyn could see the curiosity glinting in his eyes. With a chuckle, she glanced towards her brother and then smiled.

"Are you going to tell him or shall I explain?"

Lord Fairchild sighed and rolled his eyes before sitting down heavily in a chair. "My *darling* sister is just as she has always been, Waverley. I am sure you know what I mean by that."

Light came into Lord Waverley's eyes, and he smiled warmly. "Ah. You mean to say that you have continued with your reading and the like, Rosalyn?"

"Indeed I have." Drawing herself up in her seat, she sent her brother a supercilious look. "Much to my brother's displeasure, I might add."

Lord Waverley's eyebrows lifted. "And what troubles you about that, my friend? I have always thought Rosalyn a most excellent young lady."

"Even with her learning?"

The slight sneer in Lord Fairchild's voice made Rosalyn scowl, but Lord Waverley nodded fervently.

"Yes, of course! I do not think it is any gentleman's desire to have an ignorant young lady in their home, is it?"

Rosalyn could see from the way her brother's chest puffed out that he was about to go into the specific details as to why he did not find that notion particularly delightful and all the difficulties that Rosalyn's bluestocking ways were causing him, and thus, she spoke before he could.

"You have always been *most* understanding, Waverley. Now, tell me, are you in London for the Season for any specific purpose?" She grinned at him as he looked away, seeing the color in his cheeks. Evidently, he understood precisely what it was she was asking but mayhap he did not want to answer.

"Although I know that I must soon marry, I am afraid that my purpose here in London this Season is not to find a bride," he told her, though strangely, this statement made Rosalyn's heart leap up as if she was rather pleased about this. "I am here mostly to bring a little happiness to my mother, though I also am eager to see just how little the *ton* thinks of me! That might give me a little hope or a little despondency for the future... I shall have to wait to see which."

"I am sure you will have plenty of hope, come the end of

your time in London," she said, firmly. "Society will soon see that you are not at all as your father was."

"I must pray it will be so." He smiled at her, the light still lingering in his eyes and Rosalyn returned it with a smile of her own, truly glad to be in his company again. They had known each other since childhood, with his mother and their own being very dear friends. That friendship had meant a good many weeks in each other's company over the years, making Rosalyn think very affectionately of him indeed.

"Your own dear mother is not yet in London, I hear," Lord Waverley said, as the maid brought in a tray of refreshments. "Though is she soon to join you?"

Rosalyn nodded. "Mama went to spend some time with her sister before coming to London. We expect her in a month or so, though I will not be surprised if she stays in Wales a little longer! I know how fond she and my aunt are of each other. Though if she hears that your mother is in London, then that shall spur her on, I am sure!"

Lord Waverley nodded. "I know her letters have been a great comfort to my mother. You and your family have always been so very kind."

"You shall have to come to dinner soon," Rosalyn told him as her brother nodded. "That will help your standing in society. And why do you not host your own dinner thereafter? I am certain that will be good for your standing also!"

Running one hand over his chin, Lord Waverley considered this. "I suppose I might do such a thing, yes." His gaze went from Fairchild to Rosalyn and then back again. "And you, Fairchild? Are you here in London for any particular reason or is Rosalyn's standing in society your only concern?"

With a laugh, Lord Fairchild nodded. "Yes, yes. I am here

to find a bride, as I must. My mother almost continually reminds me of my duty and therefore, wearied as I am by her words, I have determined to do as is asked of me."

"And you, Rosalyn?"

"My brother thinks that it will be quite impossible for me to find a suitable match," she told him, throwing her brother a sharp look. "But I am determined to be just as I am, and I have no desire whatsoever to be as society expects or demands. If I am to make a match, then it will be with a gentleman who not only cares for me but is supportive and understanding of my interests; someone who does not think poorly of me because I am considered a bluestocking."

Her brother snorted and shook his head. "I have told her that there are very few gentlemen who would *ever* consider a bluestocking but she will not listen."

Looking back at Lord Waverley to see what he would say, Rosalyn's heart quickened. Would he too have the same opinion as her brother? She had always valued his thoughts but in this situation, she wanted him very much to tell her the *opposite* of what Fairchild had said.

Then, he shrugged his shoulders lightly and smiled at her. "I think, Rosalyn, that you should be just as you wish," he said, clearly heedless to her brother's snort of ridicule. "You are quite right to do so. If you are to make a suitable match, then the gentleman in question will need to know you, will he not? And it is not as though pretending you do *not* love to read and to learn will be a good thing!"

"Why not?" Lord Fairchild threw up his hands. "That is precisely what I have suggested and she will not have it!"

"Because how can one make a suitable match when one cannot truly know the other?" Lord Waverley asked, his tone quiet and his eyes gentle. "That would do no good at all. Rather, though it might bring a suitable marriage, it will not bring happiness with it."

Rosalyn's heart warmed. "Precisely."

Instead of agreeing with her, however, instead of even seeming to think about what Lord Waverley had said, Lord Fairchild made a dismissive exclamation and shook his head.

"I think one needs to know how to behave properly and that is all," he said, firmly. "A suitable match needs nothing more than that."

"I heartly disagree," Rosalyn answered, though her brother only rolled his eyes at her again.

"As do I." With a wink, Lord Waverley grinned at her, then turned his attention back towards Lord Fairchild. "Tell me about the young ladies you have been pursuing, Fairchild. That will take your thoughts from your present frustrations, I am sure."

As Rosalyn listened to the conversation, getting to her feet so she might pour the tea, she considered why it was her heart had leapt in such a strange fashion when she had heard him say he would not be pursuing any young ladies this Season. Did she not want the best for him? Did she not want to see him happy? Yes, she concluded, she did... so why was it she had seemingly been delighted to hear he would not be seeking out matrimony this Season?

4

Walking into Almacks, Phillip did his best to keep his head held high and a small smile pinned to his face. He had not had any intention of coming here this evening but upon his return home, his mother had informed him that she already had two tickets for the evening ball. It was not as though he could refuse to attend with her, for the smile on her face at the notion had been too bright and beautiful for him to ignore.

At least she is finding London a delightful place, he thought to himself, glancing behind him and seeing her surrounded by three ladies and two gentlemen who were all listening to whatever it was she had to say. *I am glad for her at least.*

Having no expectation of being universally accepted, Phillip took a drink from the table and then meandered to where he might stand, apart from everyone else but in clear view of all that was going on. He was sure that no one would wish to dance with him this evening – in fact, no one might even be willing to *speak* with him, and if that occurred, then he would have no choice but to return home.

Though Fairchild and Rosalyn are here, he reminded himself. *I shall not be entirely alone.*

"You are standing alone, I see."

Phillip did not move, giving the approaching gentleman a sidelong glance, his heart sinking.

"It is probably best, given that none will want you here," Lord Hemmingway continued, with a sly smile. "You *are* aware what is being said of you, are you not?"

"I do not have any interest in what is being said of me," Phillip answered, sharply. "Nor do I have any interest in your company."

Lord Hemmingway reared back as though Phillip had done a great deal to upset him. "I beg your pardon?"

Phillip frowned, keeping his gaze away from the gentleman and instead, fixing it straight ahead of him. "You heard what I said, Lord Hemmingway. I am quite contented on my own."

The gentleman, instead of moving away, came to stand directly in front of Phillip, so that he had no choice but to look at him. "Oh, but you see now what you have done? You have just confirmed, not only to myself but also to those nearby, that you are rude and displeasing in your character."

A weight sank into Phillip's stomach but he ignored Lord Hemmingway's remark, taking his gaze away from the fellow. For whatever reason, this gentleman appeared to be quite determined to injure Phillip any way he could. Mayhap he simply delighted in rumor and gossip and *that* was his sole reason for doing so.

"I highly doubt that you will have any good company this evening, Lord Waverley," the gentleman finished, his lip curling into a sneer. "Though your very presence will be spreading yet more gossip which, I suppose, shall be good for those of us who enjoy such a thing! I myself will delight in telling my acquaintances about how you stood in the shadow, unnoticed by everyone and never once standing up with a single young lady."

"I think that telling lies is a great sin, is it not?"

A cool, clear voice from behind Lord Hemmingway made the gentleman start and he turned quickly, just as Lady Rosalyn moved forward. With her, however, were some of the other young ladies that Phillip had met that very afternoon, though he did not know any of their names.

"Why, the Marquess of Waverley is to stand up with all of us," said one of the other ladies, looking directly at Lord Hemmingway with one eyebrow gently lifted. "Five dances in an evening is nothing to be disregarded, is it? I presume that, in speaking so, you have at least five dances already secured, yes?"

Lord Hemmingway opened and closed his mouth, his eyes going from one face to the next as he tried to come up with an answer. Phillip could not help but smile, seeing how Lady Rosalyn's face flushed as she narrowed her eyes at Lord Hemmingway. She was just as kind as she had always been, it seemed, though this time, *he* was the recipient of her good nature... and how much he valued her for it!

"If you have nothing worthwhile to say, Lord Hemmingway, then might I ask you to take your leave? We should all like to be in conversation but we have no desire for you to be a part of it." Lady Rosalyn, with a sniff, turned her back on the gentleman and as she did so, the other young ladies followed suit, leaving Lord Hemmingway, mouth agape, to stand and stare in clear astonishment at what had taken place.

"You *are* going to have to dance with all of us now, I am afraid." Lady Rosalyn's eyes twinkled at him as Phillip smiled back at her. "I am sorry for saying such a thing without your consent, but I could not bear to hear that gentleman speak with such arrogance!"

"You have come to my defense, and I am grateful for it." Phillip smiled at them all. "I confess that all that Lord Hemmingway said, I feared it would, in fact, take place. I was not at all certain about coming to Almacks but my mother procured tickets and thus, we are both now in attendance! Though," he said, a little more quietly, "she is happy and therefore, I am happy."

"You are always so considerate." For a moment, Lady Rosalyn put one hand on his, only to release it and then gesture to her friends. "Might I make the introductions?"

Phillip nodded, fully aware of the rush of heat that had flown up his arm from where her hand had touched his though he did his best not to react to it. "I would be delighted if you could make the introductions."

Lady Rosalyn did so at once. "These are my *dear* friends, Lady Isobella, Lady Amelia, Miss Trentworth and Miss Sherwood. We are all a part of the bluestocking book club also, which is why they were all visiting me this afternoon."

Bowing low, Phillip smiled warmly. "It is a delight to meet you all. I hear we are all to dance together! In which case, might I ask for your dance cards?"

He was soon presented with five dance cards, and hardly believing his luck, wrote his name down for each. "Though I do hope that you are all aware of my present standing in society?" he said, as he handed each one back their card. "If you do not desire to stand up with me because of that, I fully understand."

"Oh, tosh!" The one that had been introduced to him as Lady Amelia flapped one hand at him. "We do not care what society thinks, Lord Waverley. Given that so many of our acquaintances believe that bluestockings ought to be ignored or even worse, ridiculed, it is not as though we are eager to hear what they have to say about anyone else!"

Phillip nodded, just as Lady Rosalyn touched his arm again, to catch his attention.

"I did tell them a little," she said, in a voice so quiet, only he could hear. "I am sorry if I ought not to have done but – "

"You have done everything well," he interrupted, settling his hand over hers as his heart roared furiously. "This evening has been turned quite on its head because of you. I am thankful for your endeavors on my behalf."

The smile on her face lit up her blue eyes, the gentle curls at her temples gleaming like gold. Phillip took in her heart-shaped face, the fullness of her lips and the curve of her neck and felt his whole being burn with a sudden, furious desire to bend his head and kiss her – and he quickly stood tall and turned to face the other ladies.

"I am thankful to you all for being willing to stand up with me," he said, aware of the thumping of his heart. "It is very good of you."

"And I shall introduce you to Lord Albury," Miss Trentworth said, quickly. "He is an excellent sort and will not go along with anything that the *ton* say, I assure you."

"My brother and I are to host a dinner soon and Lord Waverley will join us there too," Lady Rosalyn added. "I am sure that being introduced to Lord Albury this evening will be a great help in that too."

"And I have every intention of hosting a dinner myself thereafter," Phillip finished, as the ladies all smiled back at him. "You have all inspired me now to push on, to ignore what society thinks *and* what they say. I am not what so many say of me and I shall prove it." With a broad smile on his face and a fresh hope in his heart, Phillip took in a deep breath and set his shoulders. The appearance of Lady

Rosalyn by his side had changed everything and Phillip was determined that, whatever he faced this evening, he would do so with a clear intention to prove to them all that he was *not* his father.

"I DID NOT EVEN *THINK* – "

"You are not about to apologise for dancing the waltz with me, are you?"

Phillip bowed towards Lady Rosalyn as the music began, stepping forward to take her into his arms. "I was about to, yes."

"But why?"

"Because," he said, aware of the delight in his heart that *he,* rather than any other gentleman, was dancing with her even though that was what he was attempting to apologise for. "Because you ought to be doing your utmost to find a suitable match, yes? And dancing with me means that you cannot dance with any other gentlemen – and I am sure there will be many gentlemen a little envious of me now."

At this, she let out a quiet laugh though the sound was carried away as he began to spin her around the floor. Her eyes dancing, she squeezed his hand gently.

"You are very kind to say so, Waverley, but did you not hear my brother's complaint? He knows that I am a bluestocking and so do a good many of the *ton*. Not all of them think as highly of such a thing as you do."

"Nonetheless, I am absolutely certain that there will be *many* gentlemen interested in furthering their acquaintance with you," he said, firmly, the music carrying them along. "You are quite lovely, Rosalyn, you need not think you are not in the least bit desirable because you are a bluestocking." The words came from deep within his heart and, though he felt himself a little embarrassed at speaking so vulnerably, he continued. "Not every gentleman in London thinks poorly of bluestockings, that is the truth. Do not doubt it."

Lady Rosalyn smiled up at him. "Should you like to convince my brother of that, Waverley? It is tiring to hear him complain about me over and over again."

Sympathy pressed into his heart. "I shall do my best, given that you are doing so much for me."

"That is because you are like family to me and family must always protect and support one another."

Her answer, though beautifully said and, Phillip had no doubt, said with every ounce of meaning attached to it, brought him a sharp kick of sadness. He thanked her and continued the dance though the silence grew between them instead of any further conversation.

She considers me family.

That came as no surprise, and Phillip silently berated himself for hoping for anything more. Yes, he had always been drawn to her, and yes, he had always inwardly admired her and felt an affection for her, but had he not only just reminded himself of how little he had to offer her? Had he not decided that he could not even *think* of taking a bride until he had not only improved his standing in society but also his fortune? He was foolish to think of anything more.

"Has your evening been pleasant enough?" she asked, as the dance began to come to a close. "I know you have danced but I did see you in conversation with some others also."

"Miss Trentworth introduced me to Lord Albury," he said, with a smile. "That was very pleasant indeed. I was also in conversation with Lord Mansfield, who introduced me to some new acquaintances." His smile faded. "Two of them walked away soon after, however. They were not pleased at the introduction."

"Then they are fools," came the stalwart reply. "You ought not to be treated with any sort of disparity. You have done nothing wrong."

Phillip took in a deep breath and then bowed, a little sad that the dance was at an end. "That is true, though my father did a great many wrongs, Rosalyn. I cannot ignore that. He will have stolen from some, injured others and mayhap even upset marriages." Wincing, he saw her eyes round. Mayhap he had said too much. "He was not of good character the last few years of his life. I can see why society now wishes to shun me."

"All the same," she answered, her voice soft as she took his arm so he might lead her from the floor, "it is not fair to be treated as though his sins are now yours."

Phillip had no time to answer for they were now returned to the other guests. He released her arm and she smiled at him, her brother near to where they stood.

"Thank you for dancing with me, Lord Waverley." Glancing around, she bobbed a quick curtsy, clearly aware that there would be others watching. "It was most enjoyable."

"I do not know if you ought to be dancing with him, Lady Rosalyn." A lady with a long, broad nose and eyes that were small and dark, set one hand on Lady Rosalyn's shoulder as Phillip frowned, his stomach twisting painfully. "Do you not know about his family? Like father, like son, yes?"

Lady Rosalyn's lips thinned, and she put both hands to her hips. "Lady Billington, whilst I appreciate your concern, I am very well able to determine who I ought to spend my time with. I am sure that – "

"You *stole* from us!" Lady Billington put out one thin finger, her face paling though her eyes narrowed. "My husband lost a good deal of coin one night, and it was never returned!"

Embarrassed, Phillip lifted his chin just a little. "Lady Billington, I do not know what my father did but I can assure you, I know nothing of it. However, I am mortified at his poor behavior and – "

"I have heard it said that *you* are the very same!" Lady Billington exclaimed, her eyes wide now, throwing up her hands as she stared at him. "Lord Pentland told me that you were in the gambling den with him and lost a great deal of money, though you refused to pay your vowels and are now in debt!"

Phillip's anger roared to the surface and he curled his fingers tight into his palms, trying to keep a hold of his emotions. "I can assure you, Lady Billington, that is not true. I have not set foot in a gambling den as yet."

"And why should we believe you? Your father was a renowned liar and – "

"Enough! I am *not* my father!"

The moment he said those words, Phillip was filled with regret. It was not the words that he had spoken but the tone with which he had said it. It had been much too loud, much too furious and determined, and seeing not only Lady Billington's eyes flare but also Lady Rosalyn's, Phillip realized he had not behaved as he ought. His voice should have been quiet and steady, not loud and furious. Mayhap he ought not to have said anything at all but instead, remained silent! Clearing his throat, he set his shoulders and then forced a smile.

"As I shall prove to the *ton*," he said, painfully aware of how many of the other guests around him were now fixing their attention solely to him, "I have nothing like the character of my father. Now, if you will excuse me, I think it is time to take my leave."

He did not so much as glance at Lady Rosalyn, too ashamed of his loud exclamation to even look into her eyes. With as much dignity as he could garner for himself, Phillip took himself away from her, away from the ball and, after a few minutes, away from Almacks, the shadow of his father following him all the way.

5
―――

T*en days later.*

"Dinner? At Lord Waverley's townhouse?"

Rosalyn beamed at Lady Isobella. "Yes, indeed! Our own dinner, as you know, went so well that I believe he felt quite confident in sending out the invitations. We are to attend *his* dinner this evening!" Her heart lifted at the thought of seeing him again. It had been a very difficult few days for the Marquess, she knew, for ever since the ball at Almacks, he had pulled himself away from society a little, though she could not blame him for that. She had been worried that he might refuse to attend their dinner but, much to her relief, he had chosen to do so and the evening had gone very well indeed. It had helped enormously to have had two of her friends there, as well as Lord Albury. That had made things a good deal easier for them all.

"I do hope it goes well," Lady Isobella said, as they sat

idly on the bench in Hyde Park, watching the world go by. "Lord Waverley does appear to be an excellent gentleman and I would not like him to be scorned by those he invites."

"I do not think that will occur," Rosalyn answered, having no concerns whatsoever. "He has invited friends and acquaintances who have already been in conversation with him, so I do not think there is anything to be concerned about. Besides which, if anyone dares look down at him, then I shall certainly say something! I am sure my brother would defend him also."

Lady Isobella turned her head to look straight into Rosalyn's eyes. "You say you have known Lord Waverley for a long time?"

Rosalyn nodded.

"He is a friend to you, then? Nothing more?"

At this, Rosalyn let out a startled laugh. "Goodness, no! He is like a brother to me, for we have known each other for so long, it is as if he is family!"

"Mmm." Lady Isobella said nothing more, tipping her head to one side just a little so she might study Rosalyn's expression a little more.

"I am telling the truth," Rosalyn protested, though a smile split her expression. "You may look at me with those searching eyes as much as you wish but I am quite certain of what I feel."

"Then you will not mind in the least if one of your friends thinks to pursue him?"

A rock dropped into Rosalyn's stomach. "Pursue him?"

"Yes." Lady Isobella shrugged. "He is a good-hearted fellow, you have told me, with a fine character and quite contented for you to be a bluestocking! So why should we not think about pursuing an eligible gentleman such as he?"

Rosalyn forced a smile, spreading out her hands. "I can

think of no reason why not!" she answered, seeing Lady Isobella's small smile. "Though you must remember that the *ton* do not think well of him, so that might prove a little difficult."

Lady Isobella's smile grew, a light coming into her eyes. "As you have said so many times, however, it does not matter to us what society thinks so therefore, we can have no difficulty in that!"

"That is true," Rosalyn murmured, her smile dimming. "You will also have to recall he is somewhat impoverished, though that, of course, is not his fault."

"Indeed," Lady Isobella remarked, looking away from Rosalyn. "However, I am sure that, in time, he will have improved things in that regard. And some of us have some money of our own, do we not? So it is not as though we will be utterly without coin!"

Again, a weight fell into Rosalyn's stomach, seeming to drag her down low. She did not know what to say to this, managing to only shrug and smile briefly as though this was all quite agreeable, even though, inwardly, she felt nothing of the sort.

How very strange it was to feel almost upset at the prospect of Lord Waverley courting one of her friends! She ought to be delighted at the thought, should she not? As she had only just said, Lord Waverley was akin to a brother and thus, to have one of her friends *marry* him would be a wonderful thing, would it not?

So why do I find myself so very troubled?

"I did find dancing with him to be quite delightful, though I am sure the waltz would have been even more so."

Rosalyn glanced at her friend, then shrugged as if to say that every dance was just like another.

"You will not mind if I dance the waltz with him the next time?"

"Of course I will not!" The words caught in Rosalyn's throat and she was forced to cough, though for whatever reason, this only made Lady Isobella laugh. Rosalyn was about to ask her what it was that made her smile so but at that very moment, her brother reappeared from his turn about the grounds.

"And here you are still, safe and sound." He smiled at Rosalyn and then at Lady Isobella. "Alas, we must take our leave. Have you a chaperone nearby?"

"I do." Lady Isobella smiled back at him, then squeezed Rosalyn's hand. "Enjoy your dinner this evening. I hope it all goes just as wonderfully as you hope it shall... and that Lord Waverley will enjoy the excellent company also, yourself included."

Rosalyn rose to her feet. "Thank you, Isobella. I am sure it will be an excellent evening indeed."

"I MUST SAY, Lord Waverley, you have some of the most beautiful paintings I have ever seen adorning your walls!"

Rosalyn, who was just finishing her final course, glanced with interest towards Lady Whittaker, who was speaking in the most expressive tones.

"There are some remarkable pieces there. I confess to being somewhat taken with the marble bust also."

"As was I," said Lady Coates, though her husband nodded fervently in agreement with this remark. "It is plain to see that you have a great interest in art, Lord Waverley."

"Just as your father did," added Lord Coates, gesturing towards Lord Waverley. "I was well acquainted with him many years ago and he always had a good eye for such things."

"Oh, it is not my son who cares for such things!" Lady Waverley laughed softly as Lord Waverley grinned. "Most of the pieces were chosen by myself, for I am quite sure that he would not be able to tell one thing from another when it comes to such things!"

Lord Waverley grinned broadly, a happiness sparkling in his eyes which Rosalyn was glad to see. "That is quite true, much to my shame. My mother knows a good deal more than I, and I am very grateful to her for it else my townhouse would be somewhat shambolic, would it not?"

This made all the guests laugh and Rosalyn smiled to herself, glad to see that Lord Waverley's dinner was going so very well. After Lady Billington's harsh words to him at Almacks and his response to that, Rosalyn had known the rumors would grow vehemently – and so they had. Many were speaking of Lord Waverley's dark temper, comparing him to his father and stating that they were quite sure he was just the same as he in every way, but there were still some who did not speak in such a way. Not everyone believed the gossip, thankfully, as was shown by the guests here at the dinner table. She took them all in, going around the large dining table one by one and seeing how each person had a smile on their face. This was very good indeed for Lord Waverley, she thought. An excellent night for all concerned.

"It is by Turner, is it not?" Lord Stockton, a broad-shouldered, red-faced gentleman, threw a smile towards Lady Waverley. "The painting, I mean."

Realizing she had missed some of the conversation, Rosalyn saw Lady Waverley nod. She had very little understanding or even appreciation of art, though clearly Lady Waverley took a great interest in it all.

"I thought it was!" Lord Stockton exclaimed, his eyes bright with interest. "J.M.W Turner, yes? Or William Turner, as he is known. An artist who is beginning to make something of an impression, I believe!"

"That is quite right, Lord Stockton, yes," Lady Waverley said, her voice quiet but her smile warm. "I think that particular piece quite beautiful in its own way, even though the scene is somewhat turbulent."

Lord Stockton nodded his understanding. "He often paints seascapes, yes? And landscapes also."

"Yes, that is right. The painting in question was, in fact, given to my son as a gift from his father only a little before his death, though it has been kept here in London."

Rosalyn's eyebrows lifted and she, as well as every other guest, looked directly at Lord Waverley who, with a wry smile, rubbed the back of his neck with one hand.

"In truth, I had forgotten about that," he said, his voice low as Rosalyn's skin prickled, sensing the sudden tension. "But it does go to show you how little I know of art, for I cannot even think of which painting you are speaking of, Lord Stockton!"

This made everyone at the table laugh again and Rosalyn let out a slow breath, smiling quickly at the Marquess when his eyes caught hers. Any mention of the late Marquess brought a tension to the party but the moment had passed quickly.

"Shall we take tea, ladies?" Lady Waverley was the first to rise to her feet and, with a smile, Rosalyn followed suit. "Let us leave the gentlemen to their port."

The ladies all filed out of the dining room but before

they could make their way to the drawing room, Lady Pleasance spoke up.

"Might we see the painting that Lord Stockton was speaking of?" she asked, as Lady Waverley beamed with obvious pride and pleasure at being asked such a thing. "It seems that he knows a great deal about it."

"As do I," Lady Whittaker sniffed. "I believe *I* was the one who spoke of it first, was I not?"

"You were indeed, Lady Whittaker." Lady Waverley gestured to her right. "Please, if you would all follow me, I will show you the painting. It is in the hallway, with more than a few works adorning the walls. Mayhap you will see some others that you also appreciate."

Rosalyn followed the other ladies to the hallway where not only were there paintings, there were also two marble works and a vase or two. Some, she was sure, held great value though her awareness of such things was a good deal lacking still.

"There we are." Lady Waverley lifted her hand towards the wall. "This is the painting by J.M.W Turner."

Dutifully, Rosalyn looked up at the painting, taking in the scene.

"This is the Thames, I believe," Lady Waverley explained, gesturing to the painting. "It is where it joins the North Sea, so the waves are turbulent, are they not?"

Rosalyn made a murmur of agreement, thinking to herself that the distinction between the dark clouds and the brightness of the sails gave the impression of turbulence, just as Lady Waverley had said. The sun, she noticed, was still present but covered by the darkness, as if it were doing its best to shine through them but could not succeed.

"This must be Sheerness, then," Lady Whittaker stated,

gesturing to the far shore painted in the distance. "And the River Medway."

Given her complete lack of knowledge and her less than sure knowledge of the artist in question, Rosalyn ducked her head, thinking to herself that she ought to do a little more learning about such things. Miss Sherwood, one of the other bluestockings, was specifically interested in art and the like and no doubt would berate her – albeit in a teasing manner – for her lack of knowledge about J.M.W Turner!

"I am so very glad the dinner has gone well." Lady Waverley came to stand beside Rosalyn as the other ladies moved through the hallway, looking at each piece in turn. "And that Lord Stockton took such an interest in the painting." She smiled quietly. "It means that not everyone in the *ton* will believe my son is desperately impoverished – though that is only because, I think, my late husband forgot that these things were here. Had he recalled them, then he would have sold them and used them for his own selfish purposes."

Rosalyn smiled sympathetically, having known Lady Waverley for many a year and, in that, becoming very fond of her. "It has been truly delightful to see so many appreciating his company – and yours," she said, softly. "I have been sorry to hear some of the whispers and rumors."

Lady Waverley glanced at her, then looked away. "It has been very painful, though he does not share a great deal with me. Instead, he likes to make sure that all is well with me and does not like to trouble me with *his* difficulties, though I see them all the same." She took Rosalyn's arm, patting her hand with her other one. "I am very grateful to you and your brother for your kindness and your understanding. Your brother has always been such a close friend of Waverley's, and your letters to him and to me these last long months have been such a balm in our sorrow and grief. I cannot tell you how much I am looking forward to your mother's arrival in London. Your family have been a great blessing to mine and I hope you know just how valuable you are to us both."

Rosalyn's heart filled with compassion. She could not imagine all that the lady had endured, could not think for even a moment what it must be like at the present moment for her. "I feel the very same way."

Something flickered in Lady Waverley's eyes and she opened her mouth, only to close it again and look away. Rosalyn said nothing, looking at the lady steadily and wondering what it was she had been about to say.

Eventually, Lady Waverley sighed but with it came a smile. "Waverley thinks very highly of you, my dear," she said, looking back at Rosalyn again. "He may not say it aloud but I do not think he could have had any sort of happiness here in London without the company of you and your brother. Your stalwart defense of him, your determination to encourage him into society have been noticed and appreciated."

"Thank you," Rosalyn answered, not quite certain what else to say. "I would do anything I could for your son, you must know that. He is as much a brother as my own for I think of you both as family."

Lady Waverley's smile faded just a little. "I do not know if Waverley would say the same, my dear," she said, making Rosalyn frown. "Though I do not mean that in any bad way, of course."

Rosalyn opened her mouth to ask her what she meant by that remark, confused and a little upset by it, only for Miss Martin, Lady Pleasance's daughter, to come towards them, asking a question about one of the vases nearby.

Rosalyn stepped back and allowed Lady Waverley to give her full attention to the lady whilst inwardly trying to come to some sort of understanding about what had been said. Why would Lord Waverley not see her as much a sister as she saw him as a brother? Was there something wrong? Something she had not yet seen? And if there was, then how exactly was she to approach the subject without causing any difficulty?

Still frowning as they made their way to the drawing room to take tea, Rosalyn tried to push the thoughts from her mind but the more she attempted to do so, the worse they became until she could think of nothing else but him.

6
———

Phillip looked all around the room, aware of the knots twisting through his stomach one by one. The last ball he had attended had been at Almacks, the night when he had first had to deal with Lord Hemmingway and, thereafter, Lady Billington. That had brought him a good deal of shame, mortified that he had spoken without hesitation, without being able to set a guard at his lips and had gained such a profound reaction from Lady Billington herself. He had already heard from a few of his friends that he was now being spoken of by some as a dark-tempered, ill-mannered fellow who could do nothing but rail at anyone who said a word to him that he did not much like, though there was not much that he could do about that.

"You thought it a good idea to come to another ball, did you?"

Phillip rolled his eyes obviously and turned his head away, having no interest in speaking either to Lord Hemmingway or to Lord Pentland, both of whom seemed to have an interest in irritating him with their insults.

"I am surprised," Lord Pentland said, as Phillip kept his gaze away from them though inwardly, his temper began to flare. "I would have thought after that *embarrassing* conversation with Lady Billington, you would have refrained from attending society occasions. Or is it that you hope to shame yourself still further by berating someone else?"

Phillip set his jaw tight, his fingers curling into his palms. *Stay silent. They are not worth speaking with.*

"I knew you were exactly like your father," Lord Pentland stated, as Phillip gritted his teeth, almost knocked out of his silence by the wave of anger that poured over him. "Easily angered, foolish in your remarks and, no doubt, just as heedless to the effect your actions have upon others."

Lord Hemmingway snorted. "Exactly so, my friend. Thankfully, we at least have the warning now to stay far from you, Lord Waverley, given that you are of the same ilk as your father. I am sure that the few in society foolish enough to consider stepping into your company will learn soon enough that you are no good!"

Closing his eyes for a moment, Phillip let out a long, slow but surreptitious breath. The gentlemen's insults were hard to hear and it was galling for him to remain silent but he fought the urge to speak. Doing so would only encourage them, he was sure.

"You have none of your friends here this evening, I see," Lord Pentland remarked, sneering. "You are standing alone and without company. Little wonder, for I am sure that – "

"In that, you are quite mistaken, I assure you," Phillip answered, even though he berated himself for speaking when he ought to have remained silent. "I have many of my friends here this evening and have every intention of dancing a good few dances. I am only just arrived which is why you see me standing where I am." He looked back at the two gentlemen, seeing them sharing a glance and finding the urge to defend himself growing ever stronger. "Are you come to speak with me in the hope of joining me for my next occasion? Is that what is behind such remarks? I know that you were not invited to my *very* successful dinner some days ago but I am surprised to know you would find that something of an insult given how little you seem to think of me!"

This did not seem to sit well with both gentlemen for they, together, narrowed their eyes and set their jaws tight. Feeling a good deal more confident, however, Phillip lifted his chin and shrugged.

"I do not think there is anything further to say to either of you. Kindly stay out of my company this evening, will you? I have no need for tiresome fellows such as yourselves." With that, he strode away, leaving the two gentlemen glaring after him. A sense of pride filled him, not only that he had managed to restrain himself but also that what he *had* said had been enough to push the gentlemen back! Lifting his chin, he made his way through the crowd, hoping to spot a familiar – and friendly – face.

"Lord Waverley?"

Turning, Phillip's heart dropped. "Lady Billington."

"Goodness, did you truly think that you could walk past me without even *thinking* to apologize?" Her voice grew shrill as she spoke, her eyes flaring wide. "After our last conversation, I expected to have an apology from you! I expected you to call or to write a note but instead, you have said and done nothing!"

Perhaps I ought not to have come here at all. First, he had been forced to endure Lord Hemmingway and Lord Pentland's presence and now, he was faced with the one lady he had been hoping not to meet.

"What is it you wish for me to apologize for?" he asked, wincing inwardly as she gasped, one hand going to her heart as not one but three other ladies came quickly to join her, perhaps overhearing the conversation or seeing her furious gesticulations. "I shall do so at once."

"You... you mean you do not *know*?" Lady Billington blinked furiously as if tears were coming into her eyes. "After what you said to me at Almacks, you have no regret over your actions?"

Phillip did not know what to say or what to do. He had come to the ball in the hope of finding a few friends, enjoying some good conversation, and perhaps dancing one or two dances. Yes, there were still many who did not want to have him in their company but after Lord Fairchild's dinner and then his own, he had felt confident enough to step into society again by attending this ball.

Mayhap he had been wrong.

"You are, as I have said, just like your father!" Lady Billington lifted her chin a notch, her eyes flashing as her friends began to nod and murmur, coming closer to her in clear solidarity. "He did not once apologize for what he had done. He was gleeful about it! And now, here you are without a single word of regret upon your lips."

Sighing inwardly, Phillip inclined his head. "I am afraid, Lady Billington, that I cannot apologize on my father's behalf, given that he is no longer here. However, I can assure you that I shall never behave as my father did. I shall not steal from anyone, I shall not cheat anyone, I shall not mistreat a single soul."

She shook her head. "I cannot believe that."

Biting back the words which flung themselves to his lips, words of defense against her insult, Phillip lifted his head. "I am sorry for that. Do excuse me."

The moment he stepped away, the exclamations from the ladies chased after him. He had not done anything well during that conversation and they were all making that very clear to him even as he stepped away. Groaning, Phillip rubbed one hand over his face and then began to make his way to the side of the ballroom, suddenly needing to make his way to the quieter part of the room. He had come to the ball full of hope and expectation, but thus far, it had proven to be nothing short of disastrous.

"Waverley."

He turned again, relief flooding him. "Rosalyn. How glad I am to see you." He took her in, his heart quickening. Her golden curls were coiled neatly at the back of her head, a few wisps escaping at her temples. The pendant at her neck matched the blue in her eyes, making them all the more vivid and Phillip's desire quickly began to grow, though he pushed it down as quickly as he could. "You look very lovely this evening."

"I thank you." She did not smile, making Phillip frown. "Might I ask you something?"

"Of course."

She caught her bottom lip with her teeth, her gaze sliding away. "Do you think of me as I think of you?"

"Think of you?" Phillip blinked, not at all clear as to what the lady was saying. "Do you mean that I think well of you? Of course I do, you must know that!"

"That is not what I mean." Lady Rosalyn glanced back at him, a light pink in her cheeks. "I was speaking to your mother at the dinner, and something she said has lingered long in my thoughts."

Phillip frowned, his stomach beginning to writhe already. What was it his mother had said? Surely it would not have been anything to upset Lady Rosalyn?

"I mentioned that we are akin to family, even though we are not," she said, by way of explanation. "I do not know why you would not think of me as family, but I must wonder if there is something about me that you do not like? Something about my character that displeases you?"

Thrown by her statement, Phillip opened his mouth and then closed it again, trying to make sense of not only what she had said but also what he ought to say in response. He could not say yes, he *did* see her as a sister, for that would be denying his heart but at the very same time, he certainly did not feel himself worthy of her! He had no intention of telling her that his feelings were a little more... affectionate than they would be towards a sibling, however, so did it truly matter if he did not tell her the truth?"

"You do not see me as I see you, then," she said slowly, perhaps ascertaining from his silence what he truly felt. "I thought that we were so closely acquainted that you would see me in the same light. I confess to being a little surprised at that."

"It does not mean anything," Phillip answered quickly, trying to confirm with her that while he did not see her as he might a sibling, he still cared about her a great deal. "My mother was simply stating, I am sure, that we value your friendship because it is so freely given and your devotion so strong. It is not demanded from us, as it might be if we were family. So I suppose, in that way, I do not see you as a sister. My mother was right to say so."

Lady Rosalyn blinked, her eyes glistening gently and Phillip's heart dropped. Clearly, he had said something to upset the lady though at this juncture, he was not sure what it was.

"I – I do not mean to upset you."

"But you have done." Lady Rosalyn shook her head,

dashing one hand over her eyes. "It is foolish, I know, but I thought... well, I thought that the passion I have in my heart for you would be returned."

Oh, but it is. It was on the tip of Phillip's tongue to say those words, wishing that he could express the truth of his heart but seeing just how foolish that would be to do so. Had she not only just told him that she saw him in the same light as her brother? That meant, did it not, that there was no gentle affection, as he had for her!

"I think I must step away." The smile she gave him was lifeless and dulled. "Excuse me, Waverley."

"Wait, Rosalyn!" Reaching out, he caught her hand and instantly, fire enveloped him at the touch of her hand to his, his heart leaping furiously. The very next moment, however, the fire was doused completely as, with only a look, she pulled her hand away and walked back into the crowd.

Phillip let out a low groan and passed one hand over his eyes, his heart plummeting back down again. This evening had been disastrous, for in only half an hour, he had argued with Lord Hemmingway and Lord Pentland, had then faced Lady Billington and her wrath and now, worst of all, had managed to upset Lady Rosalyn in some way, though quite how he had done so, Phillip was not certain. His eyes squeezed closed, his frame now tight with tension as he silently debated whether or not he ought to return home. Perhaps this evening was to be nothing but a failure and it would be best to make his way from the ball before things worsened.

I shall have to ask my mother what precisely she said to Lady Rosalyn, he thought to himself, snapping his fingers at the nearby footman and taking a drink from the tray he held. *I do not understand why she thought to make such a remark!*

"Waverley! Are you going to stand at the back of the room all night?"

A gentleman whom Phillip recognized as Lord Coates, one who had been at his dinner, strode towards him with a broad smile on his lips.

"Lord Coates, good evening." He inclined his head. "I am thinking about taking my leave from this place and – "

"Take your leave?" Lord Coates' smile shattered, his eyes widening. "Goodness, whyever would you do such a thing? Have you not only just arrived? You have not signed a single dance card either, I am sure!"

"I am not sure I shall," Phillip muttered, a sense of helplessness and despondency rushing over him. "Thank you for coming to speak with me, Coates, but I think it best – "

"Come now, man!" Lord Coates, seemingly unwilling to let Phillip escape, slapped him on the back. "Did you know card games are being played at present? Our host has set up a room away from the ballroom, and I fully intend to go and play for a short while. Come with me!"

Phillip hesitated, aware that his father had not only played many a game of cards but had also lost a good many of them, cheating some of the gentlemen he played with and, for others, refusing to pay what he owed. "I am not sure if – "

"Do you see him there? He refused to apologize to me, and that after nearly everyone in Almacks heard him roar at me in that furious, ungentlemanly manner!"

Hearing Lady Billington's voice and glancing to his left to see her pointing directly at him, Phillip scowled and turned his attention again to Lord Coates. "You have convinced me," he said firmly, determined now to make his way from the ballroom and all the guests within it just as quickly as he could. "Lead the way, my friend, and I will follow."

Lord Coates grinned and began to make his way through the crowd, with Phillip following after him. With every step, he felt tension coil all the more tightly within him, given what he was about to do. This was, he knew, a way to walk directly in his father's footsteps, which was precisely what he had intended *not* to do for so long – but given the disastrous evening, what else could he do? It was either this or he returned home in embarrassment and shame, and he certainly did not want that.

I will be careful, he told himself, firmly. *And even in this, I will be able to prove to the* ton *that I am nothing like my father. They will soon see that I behave better than he in everything.*

7

Rosalyn yawned as the conversation came to a close, making Miss Sherwood's eyebrows lift gently.

"Either you are fatigued after last evening's ball or you find our conversation about the artists of England and France to be very dull indeed!" she exclaimed, though there was a twinkle in her eye which told Rosalyn that she was not entirely serious. "And here I was thinking that *you* wanted to learn all you could about them!"

Rosalyn laughed softly as the other bluestockings smiled, the conversation coming to a close. "You are quite right, Eugenia, I ought not to yawn so. I have been *very* tired today. The ball last night was very late finishing. Then, I could not find my brother!" She rolled her eyes as a look of concern came into her friend's face. "He had decided to go to play cards, though he had chosen not to inform me of it. Thus, I returned home alone and, of course, could not sleep until I was sure he had returned home safely. Which he did, though he was not exactly sober-minded upon his return!"

"Oh." Miss Sherwood chuckled a little ruefully. "Then I think we can all forgive you for your fatigue. Though I do hope you have learned a little more about J.M.W Turner and his work?"

"I have indeed, yes," Rosalyn answered, with a smile. "Thank you all for your discussion. This bluestocking book club is a wonderful thing and I look forward to much to our meetings."

"As do I," Lady Amelia answered, though a tiny hint of a smile brushed the corners of her mouth. "Although I must say, I do hope that something of interest happens in society soon. I did enjoy trying to find the answer to the mystery of the necklace."

"As did I," Miss Trentworth agreed, as the other ladies nodded. "I am sure that we will soon have something, however, though mayhap it will be something a little more... banal." Her gaze turned towards Rosalyn. "Like, mayhap, a certain gentleman and the fact that we saw you so very upset with him at the ball last evening?"

Rosalyn blinked, then flushed hot. "I did not know my friends were watching me."

"Do not think that we say anything out of a selfish desire to have something else to talk about," Lady Isobella said, quickly, reaching out one hand to her. "We saw you upset, and since you have not spoken of it, we want to make certain that you are all right, that is all."

Her mouth tugged to one side as she looked from one of her friends to the next, aware that she had not said anything regarding Lord Waverley as yet. "It is a foolish thing and I ought not to have been upset by it, I am sure."

"If you wish to tell us, then you know we are here to listen to you," Miss Sherwood reassured her, "though whether our advice thereafter would be of any good, I cannot tell you!"

Rosalyn laughed at this, her heart feeling a little lighter. "It is a foolish thing, as I have said," she answered, honestly. "Lady Waverley and I were speaking some days ago, and when I said that I felt Lord Waverley as much a brother as my own, she did not respond in the same way."

Lady Amelia's eyebrows lifted. "What do you mean?"

"She said that she did not think her son felt the same way." Rosalyn looked down at her hands, that heaviness returning to her. "I do not know why it upset me so but it did, a great deal, though I did not express that to her."

"And that is what you asked Lord Waverley about at the ball?" Lady Isobella asked as Rosalyn nodded. "I am sorry to hear that it upset you, but I am sure it was not meant to harm you."

Sighing aloud, Rosalyn clasped her hands in her lap. "Yes, I am convinced of that also," she said, softly, trying to explain – when she did not fully understand herself – why she had been so very upset. "I thought that he would have felt the same way, that he *had* felt the same way for many a year, just as I have. To hear that he did not made my heart tear a little."

"Why?" Miss Trentworth tilted her head just a fraction. "Does it lessen your connection somehow?"

Letting out a sigh, Rosalyn spread out her hands. "I suppose it was because I thought our connection was very strong indeed, as strong as family might be to each other. If he does not think of me as his sister, as I think of him as my brother, then yes, I suppose that does weaken it a little. That made me sorrowful and his explanation did nothing to aid that."

Her friends glanced at each other but it was Miss Sherwood who asked the obvious question. "What did he say when you brought it to him?"

"He said that he did not see me as family because our devotion to him and his mother was so strong." Rosalyn wrinkled her nose. "That it was freely given rather than demanded, as it might be in a family group. Though I did not much care for that explanation, for it did not, to my mind, have a great deal of strength."

"Though you accepted it, nonetheless, I presume."

Rosalyn nodded in answer to Lady Amelia's question.

"I do wonder something," Miss Trentworth began, as every eye turned to her. "I wonder if, in saying that, Lady Waverley meant to suggest – " A knock at the door interrupted her and, with a sigh, she called for the servant to enter. A footman came in and inclined his head, only to look directly at Rosalyn.

"Lady Rosalyn, your brother has sent a servant to the house to ask for your immediate return," he said, as Rosalyn's heart clattered furiously. "He also said to inform you that nothing is wrong and you are not to be in the least bit concerned."

Rosalyn blinked quickly, nodding as the footman was dismissed. How could both statements make sense? They were utterly incongruent, were they not? "My sincere apologies for hurrying home, but it seems my brother has need of me."

"But of course," Miss Trentworth said, though she too got to her feet, her eyes a little more rounded than usual. "I do hope everything is all right. That message sounded a little... strange."

"It did, though mayhap my brother requires me only to

find a cool compress for his head as he faces the consequences of too much liquor," Rosalyn answered, managing to smile despite the worry growing in her heart. "Thank you all. I hope we can meet again very soon."

Miss Trentworth accompanied Rosalyn to the carriage, reassuring her as they went. It did not take long for the carriage to return her to the house, though with every minute that passed, Rosalyn's heart clamored with yet more concern. Why had her brother sent for her? When she had left the house, he had still been abed! Surely nothing severe could have taken place between that time and her return? She had only been absent from the house for less than two hours!"

"My brother, where is he?" Handing her bonnet to the butler, Rosalyn took in a slow, calming breath as he directed her to the drawing room. Without another moment, she gathered her skirts and hurried to the room, pushing open the door and stepping inside, fearful of what she would discover.

"Ah, Rosalyn. There you are."

"Daniel." Using his Christian name such was her worry, she came quickly towards him. "What is wrong? Why did you send for me?"

"It was at my request."

She spun around, her eyes flaring wide at the sight of Lord Waverley. With her mind and her gaze fixed solely on her brother, she had not seen him sitting there. "Waverley?"

He smiled but there were heavy bags around his eyes, and his face was pale. "I am sorry to send for you, my dear Rosalyn, but I think, yet again, I require the help and assistance of both yourself and your brother."

"You do?" Her breathing grew a little calmer as she

looked from her brother to Lord Waverley and back to her brother again. "What has happened?"

He winced. "It is a long and somewhat embarrassing story to tell, Rosalyn, but in short... " Taking a breath, he looked straight into her eyes. "My J.M.W Turner painting has been stolen."

8

Earlier that day.

Phillip awoke to the sound of someone groaning, only to realize that *he* was the one making that sound. He pushed himself up on one elbow, feeling the softness of the bed beneath him and struggling not to give in to the urge to drop his head back down onto the pillows again.

"My lord?"

Blinking to clear his vision, Phillip tried to speak but he could only whisper, such was the tightness of his throat. "Yes?"

"The breakfast tray, my lord. I took the liberty of preparing it before I brought it to you. Your mother is still abed but she will break her fast soon. I thought it best to wake you before she rose, given the present state of things."

"I thank you." He did not know what the butler meant but given the weariness of his mind and body, he did not immediately begin to ask questions. His face burned with shame as though the butler and the maid, who was standing to one side with the tray in her hands, were both gazing down at him with contempt in their eyes. It was not the first time his staff had seen him in such a way, he knew, but all the same, he did not much like it. Slowly pushing himself up to a sitting position, he waited until the butler had set the pillow behind him before the maid handed him the tray. Scuttling off without a further glance in his direction, Phillip was left alone with the butler who, after a moment of silence, cleared his throat.

"Forgive me for my questions, my lord, but I must ask if you would be happy for us to remove your final guest from the house?"

"My final guest?" Repeating this, Phillip closed his eyes and leaned his head back against the pillows. "Is this what you mean by the present state of things?"

The butler cleared his throat and then snapped his heels together. "My lord, the drawing room and dining room are all in need of... being righted given last evening's entertainments. I hope you did not mind the footmen helping you to your bedchamber. It was under my instruction, for I did not think that sleeping on the floor of the library would be very comfortable for you."

Feeling utterly at a loss, Phillip shook his head. "I do not recall what I did or who was present. I did not know I even had guests!"

"You had six guests, my lord." The butler did not sound as though he were judging Phillip's lack of awareness, though Phillip's embarrassment grew all the same. "Lord Fairchild was the second-to-last present, but he returned home a few hours ago. Lord Coates is still present, however, asleep on a *chaise longue*."

Groaning, Phillip rubbed one hand over his eyes.

"His carriage is ready and waiting, my lord. It will not take more than a few minutes, and it would be best to do so as soon as possible. We do not wish for Lady Coates to become alarmed when she awakens and finds her husband absent."

Opening his eyes, Phillip nodded, wincing at the spear of pain that lanced through his forehead. "Of course. At once, then."

The moment the butler left, Phillip dropped his head into his hands, trying to recall anything about the previous evening. He remembered that he had gone with Lord Coates to play cards, but what had happened thereafter? Shaking his head – and then instantly regretting his action – Phillip closed his eyes tightly, recalling how glasses of whisky or brandy had been pressed into his hands. Perhaps the gentlemen he had been playing cards with had wanted him a little befuddled so they might take advantage of him in some way.

Or mayhap, my dark mood made me careless.

Picking up a piece of toast, Phillip took a bite and chewed carefully, relieved when his stomach did not instantly rebel. What had happened last evening? Why ever had he been so foolish? It had been utterly nonsensical for him to have let himself behave so! Had he not reminded himself, as he went, that he had to be nothing like his father? And yet, in drinking far too much liquor, that was precisely what he had done.

Shame-faced, Phillip picked at his breakfast tray; the coffee and the food were helping him recover a little. Setting it aside, he swung his legs around and stood up, groaning aloud when the pain in his head redoubled itself. It was his own fault, however, and he had no intention of complaining about it. He had chosen to do this and, therefore, he had no one to blame but himself.

A knock came though Phillip did not immediately answer it, a little mortified still at the state he found himself in. He was only in his shirtsleeves, reaching to put on something a little more presentable before calling for the butler to enter.

"Lord Coates has taken his leave, my lord." The butler came a little closer into the room as Phillip grunted his understanding. "However, there is something I wish to speak with you about."

"Oh?" Phillip glanced at him before making his way to the mirror, taking in his pale skin and heavy eyes. "Is there another gentleman hidden somewhere in the house?"

The butler hesitated. "No, my lord," he said, slowly. "It is only that something is missing."

"Missing?" Phillip turned bodily to look directly at his butler. "What do you mean, missing?"

The butler looked down at the floor for a moment, then back up towards Phillip, his hands held tightly together in front of him. "My lord, it seems that one of your paintings is missing."

It took Phillip a few seconds to understand what the butler meant, his mind feeling sluggish and weak. "Paintings?"

"From the hallway," the butler clarified. "I am sorry to say but it has been taken clean off the wall and we simply cannot find it anywhere."

Instantly more awake, Phillip ignored the pain in his head and gestured to the door. "Show me." The butler turned on his heel and Phillip followed after him, wondering what could have become of this painting. Evidently last night had been somewhat raucous so, Phillip considered, it might well have been that one of his guests, whoever they had been, had thought to take the painting down to admire it and had, thereafter, left it somewhere else. Mayhap he himself had done it! Silently berating himself for being so foolhardy, Phillip slowed his steps as they approached the hallway, looking from one painting to the next, seeing that the marble busts and the vases had not moved an inch. That in itself was something of a relief, for if the busts and vases had broken then that would have been an expensive loss! Phillip had often wondered why his father had never sold these things in lieu of his lack of funds but, as his mother had once suggested, it might have simply slipped his mind given how often it had been addled by liquor.

"This one, my lord."

Phillip stopped still and looked at the empty space on the wall. It only took him a second to realize which one it was, his heart slamming hard into his chest as he caught his breath.

"The Turner painting is it not?" he asked, as the butler nodded. "The one that was noticed by some of my dinner guests."

"The very same, my lord." The butler spread out his hands. "What am I to do?"

Taking in a deep breath, Phillip thought quickly. "Given my unexpected guests last evening, I am sure that you have more than enough on your hands to have this house turned back into presentable condition. I shall deal with this." When the butler only nodded, Phillip winced, wondering just how much of a state the house had been in. "Might I also enquire of you as to who all I had at this house last evening?"

"Six guests, my lord. Lord Fairchild and Lord Coates, as I said."

"And the others?"

The butler began to tick off on his fingers. "Lord Stockton, Lord Haverstock, Lord Whittaker and Lord Raleigh." He paused, frowned and then nodded. "Oh, I forgot Lord Mansfield. He came with the other guests but did not linger for as long."

"I thank you." Phillip rubbed one hand over his eyes again, feeling them hot and gritty. "I must take my leave. Lord Fairchild may remember more than I and might know what has happened to this painting."

With an inclination of his head, the butler stepped away. "I shall have the valet sent to you immediately, my lord."

Phillip, praying that his mother would not rise until the house was returned to its proper order for fear that he would have her upset to deal with. He hurried back to his bedchamber. Surely nothing could have happened to his painting, he thought, as he took his shirt from his shoulders. It must have been misplaced, though quite why someone would take it from the wall, Phillip could not imagine.

And it was being heavily admired when I had my dinner, he reminded himself, a frown beginning to burrow into his features. *Surely someone would not have taken it for themselves... would they?*

"My J.M.W painting has been stolen." Looking straight into Lady Rosalyn's eyes, Phillip found himself struggling to hold her gaze, seeing the shock lingering in her expression. "When I first came to speak with your brother, I felt quite sure that it had only been misplaced but now, after discussing it with him, I believe it has been taken."

"But why?" Lady Rosalyn did not ask any questions as to what had taken place the previous evening, much to his relief. Indeed, there appeared to be no tension between either of them at all. "Why would someone take your painting?"

"It is the one that was discussed at length at Waverley's dinner party," Lord Fairchild reminded her. "You went to see it with all of the ladies, did you not?"

With a quiet gasp, her eyes rounded as she nodded.

"My mother told me thereafter that Lady Whittaker was *very* eager to remind everyone that *she* was the one who knew a great deal about it." Phillip shrugged. "I do not know if that means anything."

"I cannot say for certain," Lady Rosalyn said, slowly, her eyes thoughtful. "What I *would* say is that she was mostly interested in making sure that the other guests knew of her knowledge of the painting, rather than being interested in the painting itself." A few lines drew themselves over her forehead. "Was Lady Whittaker at your house last evening, then? I presume this was after the ball."

Heat rose in Phillip's face. "No, she was not," he answered, quickly. "I did not have any ladies present, only gentlemen." Aware that he would have to tell her the truth at some point, he glanced at Lord Fairchild. "Your brother, as well as some other acquaintances, came to my townhouse once we had finished playing cards at the ball. I am afraid I cannot give you any particular details about what happened thereafter. I awoke to the butler informing me that both the dining room and drawing room would need to be set to rights before my mother rose to break her fast." He watched as her eyebrows rose even higher, only for color to flood her cheeks as she looked away from him. Shame coiled like a snake in his belly, threatening to strike at him with even greater mortification at any moment. Here he was, telling the lady who had done nothing but defend him and support him in these last few weeks in London that he had acted without sense and, in doing so, had lost something valuable.

"I can say a good deal more," Lord Fairchild said,

directing his words to his sister. "I confess that I am a little surprised you do not remember anything, Waverley. You were not imbibing that much!"

Phillip blinked, surprise filling him. "Are you sure? I do recall a glass or two of brandy being offered me."

"Yes, yes, I am quite sure." Lord Fairchild frowned, rubbing one hand over his chin. "That is why I say I am surprised, for I would have expected you to recall more than I!"

"Unless," Lady Rosalyn said, slowly, "this was part of a plan."

Unsure as to what she was saying, Phillip looked back at her quickly. "What do you mean?"

Her brow furrowed. "I am not at all suggesting that I have the right answers and I might well be wrong in what I am saying but, given what we know of you, Waverley, my brother's surprise is quite understandable. You are not the sort to lose yourself in liquor."

Phillip closed his eyes and sighed. "Except I was not in the best frame of mind last evening, Rosalyn. I had something of a disastrous evening and was thinking of returning home. When Lord Coates came to ask me to play cards, I hesitated given the reputation of my late father but, hearing Lady Billington directing her fierce words towards me again, I decided to accept his offer. Given the weight of my heart and mind, I confess that I would not be in the least bit astonished if I *had*, in fact, given in to drinking more than I ought."

Lady Rosalyn did not immediately respond. Her eyes searched his, perhaps aware that something of what he spoke of had been the strange conversation between them both. Then, she gave him a small smile and shook her head.

"Let us say that you were not as foolish as you believe

yourself to be," she said, with a light gleam in her eye. "Let us say that you did not drink as much as you believe you did. Why, then, would you have no recollection of what took place?"

Lord Fairchild's swift intake of breath spoke of his understanding at the very same time as Phillip's mind took a hold of it also. "My dear sister, are you suggesting that someone administered something to Waverley?"

"It is a possibility, is it not? Someone who wanted to take the painting and found themselves with ample opportunity?"

Immediately, Lord Fairchild shook his head. "No, that cannot be. We were all in the same rooms together, of that I am quite sure. Lord Mansfield left very quickly, determining to make his way to Lord Lymington's abode for *his* card game. No-one else left." He frowned hard, his eyes going to the floor at his feet as he tried to remember something. "Wait. When I settled into a chair in the drawing room – the place I woke from, I confess – I do not remember seeing you present. Everyone else was there but you were not."

Phillip swallowed hard, wishing that he could remember more of the evening. "The butler informed me that I was taken to my bedchamber from the library."

"The library?" Lady Rosalyn's lips curved, a spark of humor in her eyes. "You wished to read despite your guests?"

The laugh caught in his throat as Lady Rosalyn's expression changed in a single second, her eyes rounding, her hand flinging out towards him. "Wait a moment!"

Phillip's stomach twisted. "What is it?"

For a few seconds, she did not speak, only to nod quickly as if she had silently determined something. "You said a few minutes ago that the butler had to set the drawing room and dining room to rights, did you not?"

"He did."

"And yet," Lady Rosalyn said, speaking quickly now, "you were found in the library. Did he mention that the library itself would require any attention?"

Phillip shook his head, holding her gaze as he began to understand her quick thinking.

"Then I think you must first ascertain whether or not the library was in as bad a state as the other rooms," she continued, her voice firm as she sat forward on the edge of her chair. "If it was not, then there is a reason that you were found there while your other guests were in the drawing room and dining room."

The realization that he might well have been drugged in some way sent a cold shiver down Phillip's spine. He swallowed once, twice and then, putting his elbows on his knees, sank his head into his hands.

"I will be able to help you, I am sure," Lord Fairchild murmured, though that instantly made Phillip lift his head. "I will do whatever I can to return your painting to you. I know it is worth a good deal and you will not want it to remain lost!"

Phillip, rather than acknowledging this, looked to Lady Rosalyn. She was gazing at her brother and the sadness in her eyes was obvious. It mayhap had not been Lord Fairchild's intention to exclude her but he had done so nonetheless, making out as though she was not worth including in this difficulty.

"Rosalyn?"

When she looked at him, Phillip was sure he saw a glimmer of tears in her eyes.

"You will help me also, will you not?"

In an instant, a big, bright, beautiful smile spread right across the lady's face, the dampness in her eyes receding. "Of course, if you should like me to."

"I do, very much," he told her, seeing, out of the corner of his eye, Lord Fairchild frown. "You were the one to suggest that there was more than just liquor involved. You were the one who saw the concern around the library. You have a sharp mind, Rosalyn, I have always known it. If you will help me, then I shall be forever grateful."

"Then I should be delighted," she answered, her smile still as bright as before. "Might I tell my friends of this situation also? They are very discreet and will be able to offer their own thoughts."

"The bluestocking book club?" Lord Fairchild was the one to speak first, a hint of a sneer in his voice. "I do not think that they need know anything about this!"

A curl of anger filled Phillip's heart. "I would heartily disagree," he said, firmly as Lady Rosalyn tilted her chin up just a little, in clear defiance of her brother's remarks. "I think you are remarkable, Rosalyn, and if your friends are anything like you then I shall be very glad to have you all supporting me in this."

"Then you shall have us all," she said, softly. "Thank you, Waverley. This means a great deal to me."

"It is I who ought to thank you," he answered, honestly. "I am sure we shall, together, find the truth about this painting."

9

Rosalyn walked up and down the drawing room, her mind heavy with thoughts. Her friends watched her in silence, their own considerations filling the air. She had only just finished explaining all that Lord Waverley had told her the previous day and now, silence was their considered response.

Recalling how he had not only discarded what her brother had said but also, thereafter, had spoken highly of all she had ascertained thus far, Rosalyn could not help but smile. Her brother had revealed his disinclination towards her bluestocking nature. Lord Waverley, in response, had stated clearly just how much he valued her! That had meant a great deal and she fully intended to tell him of her appreciation at some point in the future. It had, in its own way, cleared the tension which had fogged the space between them, making her forget her upset and confusion. This strange happening had certainly centered her focus!

"I think we must, at first, make a list of those who were at Lord Waverley's dinner and, thereafter, the guests present at his... unintended soiree," Miss Sherwood suggested, as

Rosalyn stopped her pacing and turned to face her friends. "That way we might well be able to ascertain who could have done such a thing."

Rosalyn nodded, though her brow furrowed at the same time. "From my recollection, there were a few names that he mentioned that were from both occasions," she said, as Lady Amelia reached to pour the tea for them all. "I would be very surprised indeed if one of those gentlemen stole the painting, however. They are all wealthy fellows and could purchase any number of works if they desired!"

"Did you not say that Lady Whittaker was the one who mentioned the painting in the first place?" Lady Isobella stirred her tea thoughtfully as Rosalyn nodded. "Then, might I ask if Lord Whittaker would be the first we might think of? After all, he was present and might think so affectionately of his wife that he wanted very much to take the painting for her."

"That is certainly a good idea," Rosalyn agreed, as the others murmured their agreement. "Though quite how we find out if he took the painting or not, I cannot be sure."

There came a short silence again as they all considered this, with the only sound the clinking of silver spoons against China cups. Rosalyn was about to resume her pacing when Miss Trentworth spoke up again.

"Remind me of who was all present, if you would?"

"Lord Mansfield – though he did not linger for long. Then my brother, Lord Fairchild, with Lord Coates, Lord Stockton, Lord Haverstock, Lord Whittaker, and Lord Raleigh."

"And who invited him to play cards at the first?" Miss Trentworth wanted to know. "Did you say it was Lord Coates?"

Rosalyn nodded. "Yes. Though according to Lord Waverley, he was the last to take his leave and had to be... *encouraged* into his carriage by two footmen. And that was only after Lord Waverley was woken by his butler, who, I think, was a trifle concerned that he ought not to help Lord Coates to his carriage without Lord Waverley's instruction."

"So then Lord Coates was seen leaving the house and would not easily have been able to hide a painting!" Lady Amelia said, making Rosalyn smile briefly. "And Lord Mansfield, if he left earlier, would have been seen by the servants had he tried to take the painting."

"It would be easy enough to confirm whether or not the painting was there after Lord Mansfield's departure," Rosalyn said, thinking quickly. "If we spoke to the butler, then he would be able to confirm when it was he saw the painting absent *and* about Lord Mansfield's departure from the house."

"And who might have been encouraging Lord Waverley to drink a glass of brandy here or there," Miss Sherwood suggested as Rosalyn ran one hand over her forehead, her thoughts growing furiously. "If it is as you think, Rosalyn, then that might tell us who it was that drugged Lord Waverley."

"Yes, indeed." Lady Amelia sat a little further forward in her chair. "Just because he does not recall anything of the evening does not mean that he was given this mixture, whatever it was, at the earliest part of the evening. He could have drunk it later on but the effect was so great, it caused him to forget nearly everything!" She smiled wryly as Rosalyn's eyes widened just a little. "I have been doing some extensive reading on medicine and the like. It is quite astonishing what only a few drops of some concoction can do!"

"Indeed," Rosalyn murmured, as the other ladies looked at Lady Amelia with interest. "Might you do a little more reading on the subject, Amelia? It would be helpful, I am sure, if we had some notion as to what it was that he imbibed."

"Certainly."

"And I can speak with Lady Whittaker," Lady Isobella said, reaching for her tea again. "My family is acquainted with hers, and I am sure I can find out something."

"Then I will speak with Lord Waverley and with his butler," Rosalyn confirmed. "Joceline, might you find out what you can about Lord Raleigh?" As Miss Trentworth nodded, Rosalyn turned her attention to Miss Sherwood. "And Eugenia, might you do the same for Lord Haverstock?"

"Certainly."

Feeling as though they had a path forward, Rosalyn finally made her way back to her chair and sat down, reaching for the tea cup that had been set out for her some minutes ago. "I am hopeful that we can find the painting for Lord Waverley."

"I am sure we shall be able to help," Miss Sherwood said, reaching to take her hand for just a moment. "It is wonderful to know that he thinks so highly of us all that he specifically sought out your help! That speaks very well of him, I think."

Rosalyn smiled softly. "Yes, it does. My brother, on the other hand… " Trailing off with a wince, she let out a small sigh. "Mayhap this will help my brother see that being a bluestocking is nothing dreadful."

"Mayhap it will," Lady Isobella agreed. "Even if it does not, you have Lord Waverley's support and his appreciation and that, I am sure, means a great deal."

As the conversation continued around her, Rosalyn reflected on what her friends had said regarding Lord Waverley. It was quite true, she *was* grateful for his appreciation of her and for his request for her aid; it not only lifted her heart but also made her own consideration of him grow all the more. She smiled to herself as she recalled his determination to ask her to help him, in clear defiance of what her brother had said. He was a gentleman of excellent character, she knew that full well.

A faint heat began to curl in her stomach as she recalled how he had smiled at her when she had agreed to help him. There had been a fierce light dawning in his expression, making his green eyes like emeralds. She had seen that light in them before, when they had danced the waltz together.

I did like that very much.

"Rosalyn?"

"Mmm?" Looking up, she saw each and every face looking back at her expectantly, her embarrassment growing swiftly. "Forgive me, I was lost in thought. Was there something you wanted to ask me?"

Lady Amelia chuckled and shook her head. "It was only to ask whether or not you thought we should ask Lord Albury for his assistance also, it was of no great importance."

"Oh, but of course, if you wish." Rosalyn smiled quickly, aware that she was sounding a little overly enthusiastic in an attempt to hide her embarrassment. "I think I shall return home now, if you would all excuse me. There is much I must share with Lord Waverley and he is, at present, in the company of my brother." She did not miss the knowing look that was sent between Miss Sherwood and Lady Isobella but, choosing not to take note of it or make any sort of remark, she rose to her feet and took her leave.

All the same, Rosalyn could not deny that there was a growing and somewhat fervent desire to be back in Lord Waverley's company again, though quite where that came from, she could not say. Telling herself that it came only from a desire to bring this mystery to a close, she shook off any lingering thoughts and made her way to the carriage.

"Rosalyn."

Seeing Lord Waverley on his feet as she entered the drawing room, Rosalyn's eyebrows rose. "Are you about to take your leave, Waverley?"

"I am, yes." He gave her a small smile as her brother remained in his chair, though it did not linger. "The painting was stolen only yesterday morning, and alas, today the rumors about me have already begun in earnest. I came to discuss the matter with your brother, wondering if I ought to refrain from entering society entirely."

"Oh no, surely not!" Rosalyn exclaimed, coming a little further into the room. "To hide yourself away would only do more damage to your reputation, would it not? For then who would be there to defend you? The rumors will only grow in number, the whispers spreading all the more, and you will be left without any good in your character whatsoever!"

Lord Fairchild cleared his throat, one eyebrow lifting. "That is precisely what I said, more or less."

Rosalyn glanced at him but then looked away, still struggling with what he had said about her the previous day. "I am glad to hear it. You are not going to stay back from society again, are you?"

Lord Waverley hesitated but then lifted his shoulders before letting them fall. "I have some more thinking to do. That is all."

That made her heart sink. "Let me walk with you to your carriage, and you can tell me about your thoughts at present." Without him even offering, Rosalyn took his arm and they walked from the room. She did not even let herself acknowledge the thrill that ran up her spine as they did so, for they had walked like this on many an occasion, and she had never felt such a thing as this before!

"The truth is, Rosalyn, I feel myself partially responsible for what took place," he said, glancing at her as they walked slowly through the hallway. "I was foolish enough to go to play cards with the other gentlemen after all."

"But there is nothing foolish about playing cards!" she exclaimed, looking up at him. "Yes, your father played cards, and yes, he did not do well, but that does not mean that you are of the same ilk!"

One side of Lord Waverley's mouth pulled upwards. "You are always so good, Rosalyn. Always trying to defend me."

"That is because I know your character," she answered stoutly. "And the rest of the *ton* should as well. They should know you for who you are, not for who they *think* you are, Waverley."

He said nothing but instead, stopped walking, turned, and looked down into her eyes, his hands reaching out to catch hers. Rosalyn looked up at him, her breath hitching at the look in his eyes. She had never seen such a look before, nor could she understand what precisely it was he felt. There was a softness there, a gentleness that seemed to reach out towards her, pulling her towards him with an ever-increasing strength. Her mouth went dry, her heart thumping wildly as she felt the urge to lean into him, to put her arms around him and let him hold her tightly.

"I did not ever mean to upset you, my *dear* Rosalyn." The quietness of her voice made her shiver lightly, hearing the tenderness there. "Whatever my mother said to you, it was not meant to cause pain."

She blinked as she tried to understand what it was he was speaking of. Her mind was so clouded by her feelings that it was difficult to pull herself out of that fog.

"I am touched by the way you see me," he continued, when she said nothing. "To know that you view me as family means a great deal. My heart is profoundly grateful to you for that, Rosalyn. Do not think for a *moment,* I beg you, that I do not feel the same way. I have a great fondness for you and an ever-deepening appreciation for our bond. Though I may not view you as I would a sister, that does not mean that there is no strength of affection there. It is only to say that... " Taking his hand from hers, he paused, then lifted his fingers to brush a tendril of hair back from her ear, making her shudder with both the astonishment of his action but also the feeling it evoked. "It is only to say that I have more in my heart for you than I think I could express." Pulling his hand back, he shook his head and then dropped it to his side, a slow breath escaping from him. "Besides which," he finished, a hint of a smile brushing his lips, "I have no sister. So I suppose I could not fully understand what it is you speak of."

Rosalyn did not know how to respond to this. She swallowed once, twice and then opened her mouth but no words came. This moment, this gentle brush of his fingers against her skin had brought something to the fore that she could not understand. It was as if a wave had towered over her and then come crashing down, sweeping her away.

"I shall think on all that has been said between myself and your brother." Lord Waverley stepped back from her entirely, putting a space between them that had not been there before and Rosalyn felt it, a cold chill beginning a slow descent down her frame. "Thank you for your advice also, Rosalyn. I know that I should force myself to return to society but the truth is, I am beginning to believe that it will not be worthwhile."

"I – I should miss you if you were to hide yourself away." Her voice was hoarse, perhaps an outward expression of all that she felt but Lord Waverley did not seem to notice. Instead he put one hand to his heart, and, with a slight lift of his lips, he inclined his head.

"Then mayhap that shall be what forces my return," he said, quietly. "Good afternoon, Rosalyn."

"Good afternoon." It was a whisper and nothing more, her heart beating wildly as she watched him walk away. She had forgotten all about the painting, about what she was meant to ask him about speaking with the butler. Even now, the painting did not seem to have any great value any longer, pushed away by the emotions whirling through her.

It was all so very strange and, Rosalyn considered, pressing one hand to her forehead, perhaps even a trifle concerning.

10

I should never have accepted the offer to play cards. Then I would not be getting the cut direct from so many.

Walking through the drawing room of Lord Pleasance's townhouse, Phillip kept his head high and did his best to ignore the sharp glances that were being sent his way. Some had given him the cut direct, turning their head sharply away and making it very clear indeed that they wanted nothing whatsoever to do with him. He was quite sure that this was due to his choice to play cards and the subsequent delirium that had come thereafter, angry with himself for his own foolish choices.

"My friend."

Relieved, Phillip greeted Lord Fairchild. "Good evening, Fairchild."

His friend's eyebrows lifted. "You have a look of worry on your face. Do try and look as though you are enjoying this evening, even if you are finding it a little trying."

Phillip glanced at Lord Fairchild and then demanded silently that his lips pull into a smile. Whether they did or not, he could not say, for it felt as though he were grimacing rather than smiling.

"I am glad that you decided to come to the soiree," Lord Fairchild continued, pushing a glass of champagne into Phillip's hand. "Lord Pleasance was at your dinner, so there was no reason for you to stay back from it."

"I do not want to bring the gentleman any sort of difficulty," Phillip answered, keeping his voice low. "I know very well that my reputation is dark enough. There will be many talking about my presence here, and I do not think any of them will be saying anything good. I have already received the cut direct from some."

Lord Fairchild shrugged. "It matters not. Besides, can you not think about speaking with Lord Haverstock or Lord Whittaker? Both of them are here this evening."

"About the painting?" Phillip took a sip of his champagne, considering. "I do not know. Part of me thinks that it is best to remain silent about it, for if I tell them that the painting is gone, then that will, no doubt, soon be spread around society also!"

His friend's expression darkened immediately. "There will be those who, of course, will then twist that into their own version of events, I suppose." He brightened suddenly. "Though you could speak to Lord Mansfield, could you not? That might bring a little more light to what happened."

"I suppose I could, yes."

"And you trust him."

"I do." Phillip glanced at his friend, then looked away. "Is Rosalyn here this evening? I did not see her when I came in." It was a sudden change of conversation, he knew, but he had not been able to stop thinking about what had been shared between them earlier that day. "I am, of course, very grateful to her and her friends for their willingness to help."

Lord Fairchild's lip curled. "You are a good deal more eager than I to accept the help of a bluestocking, my friend."

Phillip shrugged. "That is because I do not think it a dreadful thing for a lady to be so, my friend."

Lord Fairchild let out a hiss of breath between his teeth. "You are not responsible for Rosalyn in the same way I am, my friend. I am here to seek out my own match, yes, but I must also encourage Rosalyn to do the same! And very few gentlemen will have the same consideration as you, Waverley."

Phillip chuckled. "Then those gentlemen, the ones who discard her for being so learned and wise, would not be worthy of her."

At this, Lord Fairchild sent him a somewhat calculating look, and Phillip's smile faded. Surely his friend did not suspect him of anything? Thus far, Phillip had not once told his friend about his affection for Rosalyn, and he had no intention of ever doing so either! There was no need for it, for Phillip was all too aware of how little he deserved someone like her. His standing was poor, his fortune lessened, and he could not be worthy of her.

"I suppose I should attempt to be a little more encouraging." After some moments of quiet, Lord Fairchild looked away, though a muscle in his jaw worked hard in the silence that followed. Phillip said nothing, choosing to remain silent as his friend worked through his thoughts, giving him the time and the space to think.

"I could see in her eyes just how delighted she was when you spoke well of her learning and the like." Lord Fairchild grimaced and threw Phillip a glance. "She has never smiled at me like that. But mayhap there is more than mere support as a reason for that."

Phillip blinked, then frowned, not understanding what his friend meant. "I – I do not know what you mean."

"Do you not?" Lord Fairchild lifted an eyebrow, then let out a wry chuckle. "Well, mayhap that is for the best since Rosalyn... " Shaking his head, he came to a stop, making Phillip's frustration burst upwards. He wanted to reach for his friend, to grab his arm and demand to know what it was he had meant to say, but propriety restrained him. His heart thudded, and he pressed his lips flat, trying to think of what he could ask that would encourage Lord Fairchild to explain all the more.

"Ah, Lord Mansfield! We were just speaking of you!"

Any chance that Phillip had to ask a question died on his lips as Lord Fairchild hailed their friend, who turned to them both in an instant.

"About me?" he said, coming towards them both. "And here, I would have thought that you were discussing with Lord Waverley your interest in a particular young lady."

Phillip's eyebrows shot upwards. "Indeed, Fairchild?! And what young lady might that be and why have you not spoken to me of it?"

Lord Fairchild's face turned a furious shade of scarlet. "I have only been speaking to the lady on occasion; that is all."

"Lady Catherine, daughter to Lord and Lady Coates," Lord Mansfield said, with a chuckle. "Though given your embarrassment, I shall not push for more discussion on the matter. You said you were speaking of me?"

Phillip cleared his throat, pushing away the conversation he wanted to continue and instead, thinking about his missing painting. "Mansfield, I must first ask for your discretion."

The gentleman's expression fell, his eyes rounding a fraction. "Is there something wrong?"

"It is about the night we went to Lord Waverley's townhouse, after the ball. You were present, yes?" Lord Fairchild said, as a hand touched Phillip's elbow. Lady Rosalyn stood beside him, her hand now settling into the crook of his arm, her eyes fixed to Lord Mansfield.

Lord Mansfield nodded as Phillip tried to keep his heart from exploding into a furious beat for fear that she would hear it.

"You left earlier than I," Lord Fairchild continued, as Phillip fixed his gaze on Lord Mansfield instead of focusing solely on Lady Rosalyn's presence which, he discovered, was somewhat difficult to do. "You had another occasion to attend?"

Lord Mansfield's lips curved. "You are not jealous, are you?"

"No, not in the least," Phillip answered, quickly. "You had another card game to attend."

"Yes, that is so."

"And might I ask," Phillip continued, leaning in a little closer, "who was all present before you took your leave? Do you remember where everyone was?"

At his question, Lord Mansfield frowned, his eyes darting to Lord Fairchild and then back towards Phillip. "What has happened that you would ask me such a thing as that?"

"It is only that I do not remember the evening at all," Phillip answered, choosing not to speak of the missing painting as yet. "I was woken by my butler who asked if I might permit him to remove Lord Coates from the house. However, I had no recollection of anything taking place! Indeed, the only thing I can recall is that I went to play cards with Lord Coates at the ball!"

"Goodness!" Lord Mansfield's eyes flared. "You must have imbibed a good deal to have forgotten so much!"

Phillip managed a small smile, feeling Lady Rosalyn's fingers squeeze his arm lightly. "Mayhap I did. I am afraid I do not remember."

This made Lord Mansfield chuckle, though Phillip did not join in. "If you are trying to remember who was all present, then I can easily tell you. Lord Fairchild was with you, with Lord Coates and Lord Haverstock. The three of them were in the drawing room, with Lord Whittaker and Lord Raleigh in the dining room. Lord Haverstock was already asleep, I am sure, by that point!"

Rosalyn's hand squeezed his arm hard and Phillip looked down at her.

"Stockton?" she whispered, as he leaned towards her. "What about him?"

His heart slammed into his ribs. "Lord Stockton?" Returning his gaze to Lord Mansfield, he tried to keep his tone light. "Was he not present also?"

"Oh." Lord Mansfield frowned, one finger pressing to his lips. "Yes, yes, I recall now. Lord Stockton staggered in from the dining room into the drawing room and declared to us all that he had made something of a mess in the hallway – spilling half the decanter of brandy, I think, and shattering a glass with it. He begged Lord Coates to aid him and as I took my leave, the two of them went to see what had happened. I think they were hoping to summon a maid or a footman although, given the lateness of the hour, most of them had already retired, as per your instructions. The butler was still about, I think."

"And where was I at this juncture?" Phillip asked, feeling Lady Rosalyn's fingers still gripping his arm tightly. "In the drawing room or the dining room?"

Lord Mansfield shook his head. "Neither, my friend."

"Neither?"

"You had gone to the kitchens for some reason," Lord Mansfield said, grinning broadly now. "You were on your way there when I took my leave."

Phillip frowned, wishing desperately that he could remember what had taken place that night. Thus far, he could only remember Lord Coates inviting him to play cards and the subsequent game that followed, but thereafter, it was all nothing but darkness. It was deeply frustrating for him that he could not remember anything more.

"I shall have to ask my butler about that," he said, in what he hoped was a light, jovial tone. "Thank you for telling me, Lord Mansfield. It is a little shameful to admit that I cannot remember a single thing that took place after I went to play cards at the ball!"

"It happens to all of us at some time or another," came the reply, as Phillip tried his best to smile. "And do your best to ignore the taunts, my friends. The whispers are mere fodder for the gossips, that is all."

"Taunts?" Lord Fairchild asked the question before Phillip could. "You mean to say that there are those speaking about – "

"About the fact that Lord Waverley played cards, just as his father did, imbibed, just as his father did and lost the game too, just as his father did."

Phillip's stomach twisted as he went cold all over. "I did not refuse anyone what I owed them, did I?"

Lord Mansfield put one hand on Phillip's shoulder and looked straight into his eyes. "No, my friend. You gave all that was required, though in truth, it was only very little."

Relief washed over him and Phillip closed his eyes. "Thank goodness."

"You have nothing to worry about," Lord Mansfield told him, dropping his hand back to his side. "Indeed, you can respond to those who whisper about you and state that no, you are *not* like your father for you paid what you owed without question! Is that not a good thing?"

With a slightly uneasy smile, Phillip nodded. "I suppose it is."

Lord Fairchild took over the conversation, leaving Phillip to look down at Lady Rosalyn, aware that her hand had not yet left his arm. "Rosalyn. What are you thinking?"

She glanced up at him, then looked again to Lord Mansfield. "I think that he makes a very good point, Waverley. I think you have every right to play as many games of cards as you wish, and that you *can* state that you are different from your father, given that you pay your debts just as you ought."

Phillip returned her small smile with one of his own. "Thank you, Rosalyn. But I meant what were your thoughts as regards what he told me about the evening my painting was stolen?"

Her eyes rounded. "Oh." She took a moment. "I think that you must first speak to your butler about what you were doing in the kitchens and thereafter, confirm that Lord Stockton did, in fact, smash the glass and spill the brandy, as he said. Oh, and there is one other thing I must ask you."

"Anything."

A slight hesitation came and then her question. "Might I be able to join you when you speak to your staff? I think it would be a good idea to confirm with the butler that Lord Mansfield left when he stated he did *and*, to be sure, that the painting was still on the wall when he left."

"An excellent notion." Phillip settled his other hand on hers for just a moment, aware of how his heart flung itself upwards at the light touch between them. "You know how much I value your insight, Rosalyn. Even now, you noticed that Lord Stockton had not been mentioned whereas I might have forgot entirely!"

She smiled up at him. "I am sure you would have remembered, in time."

"Goodness, Lord Fairchild, I am surprised that you would permit your sister to be standing so close to a gentleman such as Lord Waverley!"

Phillip closed his eyes and made to take his hand away but Rosalyn's fingers instantly tightened on his arm, refusing to let him step away.

"Lord Pentland." Phillip glanced to Lord Fairchild and then to Lord Mansfield, seeing them both frowning. "Is there something the matter?"

"And I am quite able to make my own decisions as regards my sister and the company that she – and I – keep," Lord Fairchild said firmly. "I think we have already established this in a previous conversation, have we not?"

Lord Pentland snorted. "Ah, but that was *before* it was discovered that Lord Waverley was the sort of fellow who did not pay his debts! A gentleman who lost himself in liquor and then refused to pay what he owed!" A smug smile came into his expression, and Phillip gently took Lady Rosalyn's hand from his arm, coming to stand a little closer to Lord Pentland but, at the same time, choosing not to have Lady Rosalyn so near to him. This was why he did not deserve her, he reminded himself. The whispers and gossip might be unfair but they clung to him nonetheless. There was very little he could do about that, save from protecting her from it.

"I think, Lord Pentland, you ought to be very careful indeed what you say at this juncture." Praying that Lord

Mansfield had been correct in what he had said, Phillip drew himself up, aware of the other guests who were looking over towards them, no doubt listening to the conversation. "I should be greatly upset if you begin to speak lies about me, Lord Pentland."

The gentleman cocked his head. "Oh, but I have heard it from the very gentleman himself! The one that you refused to pay!" he exclaimed, making Phillip's heart slam hard in his chest. "I am sure that *he* must be telling the truth. In addition, both Lord Hemmingway and I were present at that game of cards so we are well aware of your presence *and* of your lack of propriety."

"That is very interesting," Lord Fairchild interrupted, standing shoulder to shoulder with Phillip now. "I was present that evening and recall quite the opposite taking place. Nor do I remember seeing either of you present."

"As was I," Lord Mansfield added, as Lord Pentland's smile froze in place. "Lord Coates, you were there also, were you not?"

Phillip turned his head, seeing Lord Coates coming towards them all. "Yes, I was. In fact, I was the one who invited Lord Waverley to the card game in the first place!"

Lord Pentland looked around as if seeking support, but no one stepped forward. "I can assure you," he said, though his voice rose higher, "that Lord Waverley did *not* pay all that he owed. I have been informed of it from a reliable source, and that – "

"This is why I have been receiving the cut direct, is it not?" A sudden fierceness took a hold of Phillip and moved closer to Lord Pleasance, seeing the gentleman's eyes flare wide. "You and Lord Hemmingway, no doubt, have been telling the *ton* that I am just like my father, in that I refused to pay any debts I owed. That is monstrous, for it is the opposite of what I did!"

The room fell silent, but Phillip barely noticed, taking in a breath but then continuing, determined now to defend himself. Yes, he had played cards, and yes, he had imbibed some. Yes, he could not remember precisely what he had done or said, but Lord Mansfield had already assured him that he had paid his debts, and Phillip was determined to trust that.

"What is it that I must do to prove myself to you all?" he asked, expanding his arms wide and looking around the room, catching sight of Lord Hemmingway, who was, at present, shrinking back from the crowd. "My father brought shame to our family name, as you all know very well. But do you not think of what pain and mortification that has caused me and my dear mother? Why, then, do those such as yourself, Lord Pentland, insist that I am not able to even prove myself? Why are you so determined to state that I am just as my father was, when the evidence in this regard states the opposite? What do you gain from lying about me? What do you gain from your twisted words? If you are seeking to bring me low in the eyes of society for your purposes, then you need not do so any longer. I already have enough to bear."

It was almost a collective gasp that came from those in the room, but Phillip fixed his gaze on Lord Pentland, a little surprised at his own reaction to the gentleman's lies, but finding himself all the more determined to prove himself in this matter.

"Lord Waverley speaks the truth." Lord Coates lifted his chin, cleared his throat and stood tall. "I was present at the game of cards. I can assure you that Lord Waverley paid all that he owed. There was not a penny missing."

"Though, Lord Pentland, if you are so sure that Lord Waverley did not, if you *do* have the gentleman who is angry and upset at not being paid what he was owed, then please, do present us with him – or even just give us his name so that we might make certain of this concern." Lord Fairchild shrugged lightly. "It is simple enough, is it not? In front of all the guests here, make your claim of unfairness by presenting the evidence."

Phillip watched as Lord Pentland opened his mouth, closed it again, and then closed his eyes, his jaw tight.

"No?" Lord Mansfield snorted. "Then take your ridiculous lies away from us all, we do not need them here. Lord Waverley has done no wrong and, in truth, ought to receive your apology."

"Will you give it?" Phillip asked, quite certain that the gentleman would not. "Will you stop speaking these lies about me? Stop whispering gossip that is entirely untrue in society? I have more than enough of my own difficulties to deal with without your darkness, Lord Pentland."

The gentleman glared at him and then spun on his heel, pushing his way through the crowd and stalking out of the room. There were a few moments of silence before everyone in the room began to exclaim over what had just taken place, making Phillip's head drop with relief.

"Well done, my friend!" Lord Fairchild slapped him on the back, a broad grin on his face. "An excellent defense!"

"A gentleman unworthy of your consideration," Lord Coates muttered darkly. "I do not like that fellow *or* Lord Hemmingway, for their inclination towards cruelty and selfish arrogance makes them, to my mind, utterly disreputable. I refuse to speak to them, refuse to entertain their company for fear of what it would do to my own reputation! Those who listen to them disgrace themselves."

Phillip drew in a steadying breath. "I could not have had the same impact without you all," he answered, looking around at all three gentlemen. "Thank you all." Turning his head in the hope of speaking with Lady Rosalyn, hoping she understood why he had stepped away from her, he saw she had already stepped away.

He missed her presence already.

11

Rosalyn drummed her fingers lightly on the writing desk. After the previous evening's happenings, she had not only had a good many other thoughts come into her mind, but she had also written a few things down. She would soon make her way to Lord Waverley's townhouse, along with Lady Isobella. But before she went, she needed to have everything clear in her mind.

"Rosalyn?"

She looked up just as her brother came into the room. "Good afternoon, Fairchild."

"Good afternoon. I – well, there are two things I wish to discuss with you. One is to inform you that… " Trailing off, he cleared his throat and lifted his chin, looking away from her. "Before you hear it from any of your acquaintances or even Lord Waverley himself, I should tell you that I have… come upon a young lady who interests me."

Rosalyn's eyebrows lifted, though she clasped her hands tightly into her lap, trying not to express her surprise.

"Do not ask me any questions, I beg of you, for nothing may come of it. I am only *considering* Lady Catherine."

"The daughter of Lord Coates?"

He nodded and Rosalyn, pressing her lips flat, forced herself not to present him with a barrage of questions.

"Thank you for your silence." His lips quirked. "You are soon to go to Waverley's, yes?"

Nodding, she looked away from him. "I have asked if I can be present when he speaks with his butler. I have some questions I want to ask him."

Lord Fairchild nodded slowly and came a little closer to where she sat. "Lord Waverley has told me, on more than one occasion, that I am in the wrong when it comes to you and all that you pursue. I confess that I do not fully agree with him but I can see just how much his interest and support in that has made you happy."

This surprised her, though she smiled back at him. "Yes, it has and he does."

"He thinks very highly of you, Rosalyn, and I want you to know that I do also, although I will admit that I have not expressed that particularly well."

This not only surprised Rosalyn but, much to her astonishment, brought tears to her eyes. Her brother must have noticed, for he took a few quick steps closer to her, one hand stretched out. Then, hesitating, he lowered his hand and shook his head.

"I am sorry I have been selfish," he said, as Rosalyn rose to her feet. "When you told me that I was, in my own way, thinking only of myself then you were quite right. I just did not want to admit it."

"Thank you, brother." Rosalyn embraced him, her tears falling but her smile warm. "I, certainly, shall be glad to no longer argue about something that I cannot step back from. I have never wanted to shame you; I have never thought that it would bring upset to our family."

"And it has not," he said firmly, taking her hands and pressing them. "It has been my own foolishness and arrogant nature, that is all." Smiling, he released her hands. "I have been impressed by all you have said and considered about Lord Waverley's difficulties. It has shown me how foolish I have been to ignore your wisdom, Rosalyn."

Tears came again but she managed to hold them back. "Thank you, Daniel."

A knock came at the door and Rosalyn sniffed lightly. "That will be Lady Isobella's carriage. I must take my leave."

"To go to Lord Waverley's townhouse," her brother said, though it was in a confirming tone rather than a question. When Rosalyn nodded, he gave her a lopsided smile, a twinkle in his eye. "I confess, I do wonder when you will come to me with all of this, Rosalyn."

She frowned, sharpening her gaze just a little. "Come to you? About what?"

"About Lord Waverley." With a chuckle, Lord Fairchild shrugged but then made his way to the door. "It is not as though I am blind to it all, my dear sister."

Rosalyn was about to open her mouth and demand to know what it was he meant, only for him to open the door and the butler to step in, announcing that the carriage had arrived for her. Her heart quickened at the gleam in her brother's eye, and though she did her best to be excellent company for Lady Isobella on their drive to Lord Waverley's townhouse, Rosalyn could not get his words from her mind.

What was it he had meant? It seemed as though *he* was not blind but she was! Butterflies filled her stomach as she walked into Lord Waverley's townhouse, a little afraid that he would see her confusion.

"Are you quite well?" Lady Isobella glanced at her, as the

butler took their bonnets and gloves. "You were very quiet in the carriage."

"I was just deep in thought, forgive me." Rosalyn managed to send a smile in Lady Isobella's direction, choosing not to be honest about her present concerns. Her gaze caught on an approaching figure and, as if she were overwhelmed with delight upon seeing him, her heart threw itself upwards.

"Lady Isobella, Rosalyn." Lord Waverley bowed low. "Thank you for coming."

"Thank you for allowing us to come and hear your conversation," Rosalyn answered, as Lady Isobella nodded. "Where would you like us to be?"

"The drawing room, if you please. I already have a tea tray waiting."

Rosalyn, grateful for his consideration, led Lady Isobella towards the drawing room, with Lord Waverley staying for only a moment to speak with the butler.

"You do seem to know your way about this house," Lady Isobella remarked, as Rosalyn walked into the drawing room. "You have been friends with Lord Waverley for a long time, yes?"

"Yes, I have."

"And I suppose you are very comfortable in his company *and* in his house?"

Uncertain as to what her friend meant, Rosalyn glanced at her but had no time to say anything more, given that Lord Waverley walked into the room. Her face a little flushed, she set to pouring the tea, accepting a grateful smile from Lord Waverley.

"The butler and one of the footmen will join us in just a moment," he said, as Rosalyn set a tea cup down in front of him. "Thank you, Rosalyn. You are always so good."

She smiled at him, only to note the beaming smile on Lady Isobella's face, as though the compliment had been directed towards her. Seating herself, she took a sip of her tea so she would not have to say anything to her friend nor to Lord Waverley, a little uncertain as to why her friend had been smiling so.

A scratch came at the door and, with a word from Lord Waverley, the butler and the footman stepped in. Both bowed and then stood with their hands behind their back, ready and waiting for the Marquess' questions.

"There is nothing to be concerned about, Belford," Lord Waverley said, directing his remark to the butler. "Nor you, Matthews. We have only a few questions about the night that my painting was stolen. Not that we are blaming either of you, you understand."

"No, indeed not!" Rosalyn exclaimed, as Lady Isobella nodded fervently. "It is because we are searching for this painting, that is all. We must know all that happened."

"The first question," Lord Waverley began, "is at what time Lord Mansfield quit the house. He said it was a good time earlier than the rest of us."

The butler nodded. "Yes, indeed it was." Glancing at the footman, the butler continued. "He left within only an hour of arrival."

"And I was here in the house, with the other guests."

"Yes." Both the butler and the footman nodded.

"Might I ask," Rosalyn interjected, "was the painting still there? Do you have any recollection?"

It took a few seconds but, eventually, the footman was the one to speak. "Yes, my lady. I remember because I was the one who cleaned up the broken glass and the mess from the decanter. Everything was in its proper place."

Rosalyn nodded slowly, coupling her hands together and putting them under her chin.

"There was an accident with the decanter, then?" Lady Isobella asked, as both the butler and the footman nodded.

"I was still above stairs at the time of the accident," the butler told them both. "Most of the other staff had taken to their bed, as per the instruction of the master." He glanced at Lord Waverley. "However, Matthews, two of the maids and myself were still present in the house."

"You say you saw what happened," Rosalyn said, as the butler nodded. "It was Lord Stockton, I believe?"

The butler clasped his hands in front of him. "The gentleman was a little merry, my lady. He did not quite manage to walk in a straight line and, in attempting to enter the door of the drawing room, stumbled backwards and dropped the decanter and the glass he had in the other hand. The former spilled the brandy everywhere and the glass shattered."

"But Lord Stockton came into the drawing room to ask for help," Lord Waverley said, slowly. "Even though you saw the situation and were present to help?"

"I went straight to find Matthews and the maids."

Understanding this, Rosalyn let silence flow through the room for a few minutes, her mind going over all that had been said. "Might I ask you, when you returned, were there any gentlemen present in the hallway?"

"Yes, my lady." The footman was the one to reply. "There were two gentlemen. When I came to help clean up, one took the arm of the other and encouraged him back towards the drawing room, as I had expected. The maids, Matthews and myself were to and fro in the house and through the hallway until the mess was cleared and the floor cleaned."

"And where was I at this juncture?" Lord Waverley spoke

in a low voice, a small frown on his face. "I was not present, I believe."

"No, my lord. You had gone to the kitchens in search of something to eat." A brief smile brushed across the butler's face. "I did state that I could wake the cook and have something prepared but you would not have it. Instead, you determined to find something yourself so that she did not have to be roused."

Rosalyn's heart softened as she thought of Lord Waverley's consideration. He was always so gentle-hearted, she thought, so kind and generous in his ways.

So why have I never considered him as a suitable match?

The thought penetrated right through her, shattering everything else that she was considering. The conversation around her, the matter of the painting and the difficulties Lord Waverley faced were all gone in a moment, leaving her with nothing more than a tight chest and ragged breathing.

"I returned from the kitchen, then," Lord Waverley said, as Rosalyn tried to think about all that was being said around her instead of her own, confused thoughts. "I had something with me, I presume. Do you know where I went thereafter?"

The butler hesitated, glanced at the footman and then shook his head. "No, my lord."

"Though you did not take the food to either the dining room or the drawing room," the footman added, forcing Rosalyn's attention back to the conversation at hand.

"No?" Lord Waverley sat forward in his chair, urgency in his voice. "How can you be sure of that, Matthews?"

The footman spread out his hands. "Because in the morning, one of the maids remarked that there had been some food left in the library from the previous evening's events."

Rosalyn snatched in a breath. The library? Thinking quickly, she looked up at Lord Waverley. "Then something – or someone, most likely – diverted you from returning to the drawing room."

"So it would seem," Lord Waverley murmured, one hand rubbing at his lips. "The only question is... who?"

12

Phillip took in a deep breath and set his shoulders, lifting his head high before he took his first step away from the carriage. Trying to gather his courage, he took all of three steps before he came to a stop again, struggling against the fear that he would be rejected utterly.

"Come now, you are not afraid of the *ton,* are you?"

Phillip glanced to his left, about to make a sharp remark only to see Lord Fairchild grinning at him from where he stood beside his own carriage. "Fairchild. Good evening." He winced. "And yes, I am a little concerned, I admit it."

"Why?"

"Do you not recall the way that I railed at Lord Pentland and, for a few moments, the entirety of the guests present at the soiree?" Phillip asked, a flush creeping up into his chest. "Yes, I have been somewhat distracted by our investigations but that does not mean I have forgotten the looks I received when I spoke."

"I do recall it and, truth be told, I think it was an excellent thing that you did."

Phillip blinked, a little surprised. "I beg your pardon?"

"Telling the *ton* that you did not deserve their derogatory remarks, their disdainful looks?" Lord Fairchild shrugged. "I do not think that it was at all a poor thing to say. Instead, I think it very good, for you told them precisely what they needed to hear. Why should you continue to be treated so? It is not as though you have done anything wrong. Besides, did you not *also* prove Lord Pentland to be a liar? Did you not also show that the truth he supposedly claimed was nothing but darkness and lies?"

Phillip considered this, then nodded slowly. "I suppose I did." He turned his gaze towards Lord Tolldark's townhouse. "I cannot know what sort of welcome I am to receive, so I confess to being a little anxious." He glanced towards Lord Fairchild, then looked away. "And I confess, I worry about what effect my presence will have upon your reputation."

"Mine?" Lord Fairchild stared at him, shock melting into his expression. "My dear friend, you cannot think that I, in any way, agree with anything these society fools say of you!"

"No, it is not that." Phillip shook his head, rubbing one hand over his eyes and silently thinking that he ought not to have said anything whatsoever, given the reaction of his friend. "What I mean by that is to state that I fear what others might think of you, should they see you in my company now. If the reaction is to be dire, then what will happen to you should you stand alongside me?"

Lord Fairchild shook his head, came directly towards Phillip, and put one hand on his shoulder. "My friend, I care not."

The response was so determined, so fixed that Phillip did not fully know how to respond. He looked back at his friend, took in a deep breath, and then dropped his gaze to his feet, the image of Lady Rosalyn rising in his mind. If this was how his friend felt, then was there any possibility that Lady Rosalyn would feel the same thing? Would she care little for his reputation and what might besmirch her if she stepped closer to him?

As if he had known the image in Phillip's mind, Lord Fairchild tilted his head, eyes fixing on Phillip's once more. "My sister feels the very same way as I, Waverley. Do not think for even a moment that either of us are, in any way, disinclined towards your company, and certainly do not let yourself believe that we are in any way concerned about our own standing when it comes to our friendship with you! You should know as well as I that Rosalyn does not care one bit about society and its view of her." He chuckled ruefully, looking away. "It would take the right kind of gentleman to see her for the beauty that she is," he continued, turning his gaze back towards Phillip as another flush began to crawl up Phillip's chest. "Someone who does not give any consideration to society, who knows the sort of cruel beast it can be, and who stays far from all manner of gossip and the like."

Opening his mouth to try and speak, Phillip was forced to clear it once, twice before he was able to reply. "You know your sister well, Waverley. I am sure you will not steer her in the wrong direction when it comes to her future."

"I shall not," came the reply, although the grin on Lord Fairchild's face told Phillip that he was all too aware of Phillip's reaction though, thankfully, he did not mention it. "Now, are you to come inside? Your invitation still stands, does it not? It has not been revoked."

Phillip shook his head no.

"Then come on in! Let us go in together, for I am quite sure that all will be well. And," he said, with a twinkle in his eye, "Rosalyn will be glad to see you. She was hopeful you would attend tonight."

Hearing this, all of Phillip's resolve grew so swiftly and with such strength, it felt as though energy infused every muscle in his body. "Then let us go," he said, acknowledging Lord Fairchild's grin but saying nothing about it. "And let us pray it shall be just as you say!"

"A VERY DIFFERENT atmosphere this evening, I think."

Taking what was his second glass of brandy from a footman, Phillip looked around the room and nodded slowly, though he did not say anything. From the moment he had entered the house, he had been welcomed with both warmth and seeming delight at his presence. It was most extraordinary and, truth be told, not at all what Phillip had been expecting. There had been smiles and welcoming nods as he had made his way from the hallway through to the drawing room, and even now, as he meandered with Lord Fairchild towards the ballroom, Phillip felt himself more and more astonished.

"They all appear very happy to have you present," Lord Fairchild continued, with a nudge of Phillip's elbow. "Ah, there is my sister."

Phillip's heart lurched but he set his face with a small smile and made his way towards her, seeing how her eyes appeared to fill with light upon seeing him.

Dare I hope?

"There you are, brother! I was afraid you had quite forgotten to attend and had left me here with Lady Shrewsbury!" She threw a glance at Lady Amelia, her eyes twinkling. "Not that I was in any way disinclined towards your company and that of your mother's also, of course."

Lady Amelia laughed softly and smiled first at Phillip and then at Lord Fairchild. "We were glad to take you in our carriage, given that your brother was to be tolerably late!"

Phillip glanced at his friend, who shrugged but said nothing.

"Ah, he has not told you?" Lady Rosalyn laughed, holding up one finger towards her brother as he began to protest. "My *dear* brother has a young lady that he is considering. They were out taking a walk before the fashionable hour, and he lingered in the park with her thereafter." Chuckling at the blush that rose in her brother's cheeks, Lady Rosalyn dropped her hand. "*That* is why he is tardy though, for some reason, he does not appear to want to inform anyone about that, even though there would have been a good many people seeing him with Lady Catherine this afternoon!"

Lord Fairchild closed his eyes and let out a slow hiss of breath. "It was just a walk, Rosalyn."

"I am delighted to hear you have taken a walk with Lady Catherine! She is the daughter of Lord Coates, yes?" Phillip exclaimed, truly glad to hear that his friend had taken an interest in a young lady of note. "That is excellent news. I do hope that you found your time with her pleasing?"

His friend grimaced but glanced towards him. "I did, though I found the subsequent questioning from my sister to be somewhat frustrating. Pray, do not begin to join her in that!"

Phillip laughed and promised he would not do so, looking back into Lady Rosalyn's eyes and finding her already gazing at him. There was a gentle smile on her lips and a question in her eyes that Phillip could not quite make out. Was she asking him about his thoughts on Lady Catherine? Or was there something more there?

"We have been doing a good deal of thinking and

discussing the matter of your missing painting, Lord Waverley." It was Lady Amelia who spoke now, breaking the silence and pulling Phillip's attention away from Lady Rosalyn. "Rosalyn has told me about what you discovered from speaking with your butler."

With a small nod, Phillip spread out his hands. "For some reason, I was distracted upon my return from the kitchens and made my way to the library." He dropped his hands to his sides. "I do not know why or who distracted me. That is the trouble."

"But it can only have been those present, surely?" Lady Amelia said as Lady Rosalyn nodded. "That is what Rosalyn and I were discussing at this very moment!"

Phillip took a moment, then nodded. "Yes, that is so." There had not been a great deal of time to talk after their discussion with the butler, and, truth be told, Phillip had been trying to understand all that had been said and explained to him. This was now the next thing to consider. "Lord Fairchild I will exclude." With a chuckle, he let the smile slide from his face. "That leaves Lord Raleigh, Lord Whittaker, Lord Haverstock, Lord Stockton, and Lord Coates."

"And did not Lord Mansfield state that Lord Haverstock was already asleep by the time he took his leave?" Lord Fairchild shrugged. "I would put him to one side, though not forget about him entirely."

"Might I also suggest that we do the same with Lord Stockton?" Lady Rosalyn suggested. "Everyone who saw him said he was deep in his cups. I would be very surprised if he would have had the presence of mind – or even the stability – to go in search of the painting, take it from the wall, and thereafter, find a way to remove it from the house."

Phillip agreed quickly. "That does make things a little

easier, though Lord Coates was the last to leave, and he had to be *encouraged* into his carriage."

"So that leaves us only with Lord Raleigh and Lord Whittaker." Letting out a sigh of frustration, Phillip shook his head. "That leaves me to consider Lord Whittaker first, then, for out of the two, he was the only one present at the dinner."

"And his wife was very interested in the painting," Lord Fairchild reminded him, as Phillip nodded. "Could it be as simple as that? He stole it to keep his wife contented?"

The entire situation did not sit well with Phillip, and he grimaced, rubbing one hand over his chin. "I am not sure. I cannot say for certain whether such a thing happened or not, of course, but surely a gentleman would not do that, no matter how much he cares for his wife?"

Lady Rosalyn smiled gently and put a hand on his arm for only a few moments. "I think, Lord Waverly, that you might be surprised at just how much a gentleman or lady would do for the person they loved desperately."

Phillip did not know what to say to this, his mouth going dry as he gazed down into her eyes and felt his heart fill with an even greater, deeper, and stronger affection for her than he had ever felt before. It was as if the rest of the room were gone, fading away into darkness, leaving only her. The urging of his friend came back into his mind, reminding him that, according to Lord Fairchild, neither he nor his sister cared one jot about what society would think of their close connection... so had he been foolish to pull himself away from her? To tell himself that he was not worthy of her?

"Shall we dance, Lord Waverley?"

Phillip blinked, coming back to himself and realizing

now that someone was playing the pianoforte as Lady Rosalyn's eyebrow lifted gently in question.

"I am not sure if this is the entertainment that was promised but it appears that a few gentlemen and ladies would like to dance," Lord Fairchild grinned, nudging Phillip out of his stupor all the more. "Lady Amelia, might you join me?"

"I should be glad to." The lady went quickly, leaving Phillip alone with Lady Rosalyn. He held out one hand to her and, with a smile, she took it. The joy that flooded him as he led her out to dance was inexpressible, and as the dance began, Phillip realized that his worry over the painting was not his biggest concern. It was, in fact, the matter of his heart and Lady Rosalyn. *It* was the greater mystery, holding the greatest strength over his mind and heart... and it was only he who could solve it and bring it to a conclusion.

Though if it would be a happy and satisfactory ending, Phillip could not yet say.

13

"You care for Lord Waverley, do you not?"

Rosalyn walked slowly down the London street, arm in arm with Lady Isobella, but choosing not to answer immediately. Letting herself consider it, she glanced at her friend before saying anything. Lady Isobella was smiling quietly, no judgment in her eyes or her expression, and Rosalyn, letting out a slow breath, finally admitted aloud all she had been feeling.

"For years, I have always seen him as a brother to me," she answered, as Lady Isobella listened without interruption. "I thought of him as I do Daniel, as if he were truly family. There has always been a fondness for him in my heart, and I have always held him in great affection. Now, however, I begin to wonder whether what my heart holds is more than I had ever thought." Her heart twisted and she looked away. "It was strange to me that my heart was glad when I heard he was not seeking out a bride this Season. It ought not to have been so!"

"And that is when you began to wonder if you had more in your heart for him than you believed?"

"Indeed." Rosalyn sighed and shook her head. "But we are thinking only about the painting at the present moment, and I am doing my utmost not to consider anything else. I cannot be sure that he feels the same way as I do! To tell him of what I feel would be a great risk, I am sure, and that makes my heart deeply afraid."

Lady Isobella's eyebrows lifted. "Because you feel that he will not return your affection?"

"Because if he does not, then our friendship will be quite broken."

"And you do not want to even entertain that possibility, even though – and I am sure I speak as our other friends think also – he is quite besotted with you."

Rosalyn's heart leaped up but she ignored it. "It could be mere friendly affection, just as I have held for him. That could be all that you are seeing."

"It could be, yes," Lady Isobella answered. "Or it could be something more. You have to decide whether or not it is worth the risk, I suppose."

With a tiny smile, Rosalyn let the remark fall between them but said nothing more, letting her thoughts catch it instead. Lady Isobella was quite right, she *did* need to decide what she ought to do – but the fear of what would happen if she confessed all and he did not return her feelings was very severe indeed.

"What do you think about what was said of Lord Raleigh?" Lady Isobella asked, changing the subject entirely for which Rosalyn was grateful. "It does not appear as though he has any interest in art!"

Rosalyn's lips pressed tightly together as she considered. They had only just come from a meeting of the bluestocking book club, where they had done nothing but discuss the missing painting. Miss Trentworth had done all she could to find out as much as possible about Lord Raleigh and, from what she had learned, he had not even the smallest interest in paintings or the like. Evidently, his house was almost devoid of them, which did not make it likely that he had stolen the painting. "I think that, if he has no motive to steal the painting, then we are, most likely, looking at Lord Whittaker as being the culprit."

Lady Isobella's lips pursed as she nodded slowly. "All the same," she said, "given what *I* know of Lord and Lady Whittaker, it seems unlikely to me that they would be involved in the theft also!"

With a small smile, Rosalyn glanced at her friend. "I know. You are acquainted with the family, and that does mean that you know more about them than I. I understand that you do not think them capable or such a thing but – "

"They have no need for it!" Lady Isobella exclaimed, surprising Rosalyn with her fervor. "That is what I am trying to say, for if there is no reason for them to steal the painting, then it must be someone else."

Coming to a stop, Rosalyn turned to face her friend. At the meeting, Lady Isobella had been fervent in her belief that Lord and Lady Whittaker had nothing whatsoever to do with the theft and yet, the other bluestockings had determined that they were still worth considering. Now, however, Rosalyn wondered if she had made a mistake in being so adamant. "If you truly believe that we are wrong in thinking it was Lord Whittaker, then that means it was someone else."

Lady Isobella's eyes searched hers. "Yes, that is precisely what I am trying to say."

"Then," Rosalyn continued, with a small frown, "we must again consider the other gentlemen."

"I think it would be wise to do so."

Rosalyn opened her mouth to say that she was still unsure that Lord Whittaker could be thrown from their considerations completely, only for something else to catch her eye. Her breath hitched, and she grabbed Lady Isobella's hand, quickly pulling her in another direction.

"What is it?"

"There, do you see?" Rosalyn kept her steps slow, her eyes fixed on the two gentlemen before her. "That is interesting, is it not?"

Lady Isobella made a small exclamation and quickly looped her arm through Rosalyn's. "We must be careful in how we follow them. We cannot be obvious."

Nodding, Rosalyn made her way carefully after them both, a little surprised when a third gentleman came to join the first two. When they stepped into a narrower street, Rosalyn slowed her steps completely, her heart quickening.

"We should go this way," Lady Isobella said, urging her a little further away from the street. "If we stand and make it look as though we are deep in conversation, then one of us will be able to watch all that is going on."

"Although we will not be able to hear them," Rosalyn agreed, a little frustrated. Coming to a stop, she fixed her eyes on the narrow street, seeing all three gentlemen come to a stop. Two of them were speaking fervently now, though not to each other. Instead, both were fixing their full attention to the third, who was now lifting his hands, palms out towards them in some sort of gesture of defense.

"Are they still there?" Lady Isobella asked, her voice a little breathless. "Can you see them?"

"I can." Rosalyn narrowed her eyes lightly, trying to see. "It does not mean anything, of course. It could be a simple conversation about something else entirely, but all the same, it is very strange indeed to see them so." She tensed, seeing the third gentleman turn on his heel and stride away from the other two, his face dark with evident anger. He made his way out of the narrow street and back out to where they both stood, and her breath swirling in her chest, Rosalyn looked away, praying that he had not noticed.

"He is gone, then," Lady Isobella whispered, her gaze going over Rosalyn's shoulder. "Are the other two still there?"

"They are, but they are talking to each other now. One is looking toward the fleeing gentleman." Rosalyn rubbed her hands over her arms, feeling a little chilled. "I think we must go to speak with Lord Waverley at once." Her eyes found Lady Isobella's again. "He will want to know what we have witnessed, for it might speak into the loss of his painting."

Lady Isobella nodded and quickly stepped away, going back in the direction they had come from in search of their waiting carriage. Rosalyn walked with her, not saying another word, as if she were afraid that the gentlemen in question would hear her. Her stomach roiled, worry flooding her. There was more to that meeting than it seemed, she was sure. There had been upset, anger, and clear dislike between the gentlemen, and given what she knew thus far, their meeting in itself did not make sense! Licking her lips, she centered her thoughts on Lord Waverley, telling herself that she would soon be with him, would soon be able to tell him all she had seen and of the troubled thoughts that now tormented her.

He would offer her that safety again, his hand going to hers, the quiet look in his eyes bringing her calm and security. Closing her eyes for only a second, she drew in air and realized the truth.

I am in love with him.

14

"If you might, then I – "

"Waverley?"

"Rosalyn?" Phillip rose from his seat in an instant, striding across the room, caught by the fear in her eyes. "Whatever is the matter?"

She said nothing, putting her arms out to him and, as though it was the most natural thing in all the world, Phillip pulled her close. His eyes closed, but he asked her nothing despite the many questions that poured into his thoughts. The butler stepped tactfully out of the room, though he left the door wide open, perhaps aware that there was a need for propriety at the present moment.

"Lady Isobella was with me, but she had to return home." Lady Rosalyn's voice was muffled against his chest. "Forgive me, Waverley, I know this may be foolish, but I have been so unsettled by what I have seen."

"There is nothing foolish about this." Unwilling to release her from his arms, Phillip closed his eyes and inhaled gently, his stomach swirling as the gentle scent of lavender caught him. How easy it would be to look down into her eyes and lower his head, leaving her to close the distance between them! He would not require any words then, would he? All he would need would be that one single moment when he might know for certain whether or not his feelings were returned.

Except she does not need that at present.

Gently disentangling himself and hating the cold that swept into him as she stepped back from his arms, Phillip gestured for her to sit down. "Should I send for your brother?" He frowned, realizing that she had come to him rather than returning home. "There is nothing wrong with Fairchild, is there?"

Lady Rosalyn shook her head, pressed one hand flat against her forehead, and then closed her eyes, choosing not to sit down. "No, it is not him. Though mayhap I ought to have returned home first, but the truth is, after what I saw, I could think only of you. I could not tell him considering what it might mean to him and all his considerations."

Considerations? "Please sit down, Rosalyn." Phillip took her arm and carefully led her to the couch so that she might sit. He did not like the way her gaze darted this way and that; he did not like how she caught the edge of her lip. "Mayhap I should send for your brother, yes? He could bring the carriage for you, could he not? We can talk before he arrives."

She nodded absently, and Phillip quickly rang the bell. When the footman arrived, he stated what was required and asked for some refreshments to be sent up quickly thereafter. Then, choosing to sit beside Rosalyn, he reached out to take her hand, surprised when she gripped it tightly. "Tell me what it is you have seen."

She swallowed hard, closed her eyes, and then let out a breath before she answered. "When we were at the soiree, the one where you confronted Lord Pentland, was Lord Coates not also present?"

Phillip nodded. "Yes, he was."

"He declared that Lord Pentland was lying about what he had supposedly heard, did he not?"

Again, Phillip nodded.

"I am sure, before I left the conversation, that I overheard Lord Coates state that he thought Lord Hemmingway and Lord Pentland to be dreadful fellows, or something akin to that."

"Yes, he did," Phillip answered, not certain where these questions were taking them. "He made it quite clear that he did not think well of them at all and stated, quite clearly, that he had no time for their company. He stated, in fact, that he refused to even speak with them!" He gave her a tiny smile. "I confess to being quite delighted at just how determinedly he set against them. Indeed, he said that those who listened to them betrayed their own foolishness! His solidarity was something I valued a great deal."

Rather than bringing Lady Rosalyn any sort of comfort, his words only seemed to upset her further. She shook her head, closing her eyes tightly as she gripped his hand.

"I do not think he can be trusted," she said, her voice a low whisper. "Oh, my dear Waverley, I have only just seen him in deep conversation with both Lord Hemmingway *and* Lord Pentland!"

Shock ran through him, spreading ice from the center of his heart outward. He tried to take this in, tried to think of another reason for the gentleman to be speaking with these two despicable gentlemen but found he could not.

"I was greatly astonished," Lady Rosalyn continued, shifting in her seat so she was a little closer to him. "You cannot imagine my surprise upon seeing him speaking with them! At first, it was just he and Lord Pentland, and thereafter, Lord Hemmingway came to join them. What concerned me the most was that they walked to a narrower, quiet street and spoke there, as if they were hiding from others."

"So they would not be seen," Phillip muttered, pushing one hand through his hair and exhaling hard. "There must be something else to this, surely?"

"It may very well be nothing to do with you," she agreed, quickly. "Mayhap there is some other reason but... oh, Waverley, the moment I saw them, great fear and dread filled my heart. These two gentlemen have been hounding you, have they not? So why is Lord Coates in such deep conversation with them? What is it that they want from him? Or he from them?" A catch came into her voice. "And what am I to say to my brother? He is becoming slowly more and more inclined towards Lady Catherine, Lord Coates' daughter! If I say anything about Lord Coates, then I am sure he will pull himself away from her."

"And you do not want that."

She shook her head, a single tear dripping down her cheek. "No, I do not," she answered, a little hoarsely. "I want him to be happy, to have a heart filled with affection for another rather than making a match out of requirement and duty."

Phillip's heart pounded as he licked his lips, trying to find the right words to say, wanting both to comfort her and yet, at the same time, stay sober-minded so he would not give himself away. This was not the time nor the place for such a conversation if, indeed, he was going to pursue it. "That is a beautiful desire, Rosalyn," he answered, unable to help himself as he reached out to brush the tear from her cheek. "Is that not what every heart wants?"

Her eyes rounded at the edges and Phillip realized, a little too late, that his hand had lingered, his fingers trailing lightly down her cheek. Dropping his hand quickly, he cleared his throat and looked away, his skin prickling.

"Waverley."

Her voice was so soft, he could barely hear it. Struggling to bring himself to look at her for fear of what he would see in her eyes, Phillip clasped his hands in his lap. "Yes, Rosalyn?"

"Is that... is that something *you* want for yourself?"

"Yes." The answer came swiftly, his eyes turning to her without hesitation now. "Yes, that is absolutely what I want, though whether I shall ever gain it, I cannot say."

The intensity in her eyes trapped him in her gaze, the sweetness of her smile like honey on his tongue. They shared not a word as Phillip's breath grew faster and faster, the urge to say something, to confess the truth to her, began to burn hot in his chest.

"Rosalyn, I must tell you..." Closing his eyes so that he might find some sort of sense in his thoughts so he would know what to speak, he felt her hand touch his again. With a start of surprise, he opened his eyes to see her leaning towards him, a faint pink in her cheeks. He could not think. He could not speak. All he could see was her, his breathing now coming to a shuddering stop as he gazed into her eyes.

"Phillip."

It was the first time she had ever said his name aloud, and it felt as though the sun had burst through the room and shone down light and heat upon him. Opening his eyes, he grasped her hand tightly with his own and let the other lift back towards her cheek, desperate now to find some sort of closure to this strange twisting, turning conversation between them.

"My dear Rosalyn," he rasped, her skin like silk beneath his fingers. "For many a year, I have felt – "

"Rosalyn?" The door flew open, and Phillip, in a single second, had not only dropped his hand from her face but had leaped to his feet, just as Lord Fairchild rushed in. He did not so much as glance at Phillip but instead went straight to his sister, sitting down in the space where Phillip had been.

"Goodness, you have come in like a whirlwind!" Lady Rosalyn exclaimed, as her brother grasped her hands. "I am well, brother, truly."

"Why are you here? Why was I sent for so urgently?" he asked, throwing a glance towards Phillip but then looking back towards Lady Rosalyn. "Where is Lady Isobella? Has something happened?"

"The refreshments, my lord."

Phillip nodded, grateful that the maid had brought about a gentle interruption to Lord Fairchild's rush of questions. "I thank you. Now, Fairchild, I can only apologize for my footman, for if he told you to come here with great speed and frightened you in that, then that was not what he ought to have done."

Lord Fairchild released Lady Rosalyn's hands as Phillip moved to pour the tea so she would not have to. "He did not say with any great urgency, no, but that I was needed here as soon as I was able. However, the fact that Rosalyn is here, alone rather than with Lady Isobella told me that something was wrong. Is it about the painting?" He looked at his sister again. "Are you sure you are alright?"

"I am." She smiled, then looked up at Phillip as he set the tea down in front of her. "Waverley was very good."

The softness in her voice made Phillip's toes curl, aware that the conversation between them had not yet come to any sort of conclusion though, of course, that could not happen now. Turning away, he strode across the room and poured two small measures of brandy, assuming that Lord Fairchild would be grateful for one.

"Then why are you here?" Lord Fairchild asked as Phillip handed him one glass. "What happened that made you come here?"

Phillip listened carefully as Lady Rosalyn explained what she had seen. Lord Fairchild's face went sheet white, only for color to slowly climb back into his face as Lady Rosalyn stated that they could not be at all sure what the purpose was behind such a conversation and mayhap she ought not to have had such a great fright over it all.

"No, I think you are right to be suspicious," Lord Fairchild, as Phillip sank into a seat, looking from his friend to Lady Rosalyn, his gaze lingering upon her. "That does seem very strange indeed."

"Though it has no bearing on Lady Catherine," Phillip reminded him, as Lord Fairchild grimaced. "That is why Rosalyn came to me rather than to you, my friend." The warmth in his heart grew. "Because she cares for you, wanting you not to be overly troubled when it comes to the lady."

"That does not matter at present." Lord Fairchild dismissed that particular concern with far too much haste, waving it away as though it were of no concern. "What matters now is whether or not Lord Coates was the one responsible and, if so, where he has put the painting."

Lady Rosalyn sighed heavily. "I was sure that Lord Whittaker was most likely the one responsible, but Lady Isobella is certain it could not be, and she is close to the family, so I do trust her judgment."

"Then we look to Lord Coates," Phillip stated, unequivocally, trying to center his mind on that rather than on what he had so very nearly shared with Lady Rosalyn. "And somehow, we not only seek to discover if he *did* steal the painting but also for what purpose."

"And where he put it," Lord Fairchild muttered, before taking a sip of his brandy. "He was the last one to leave your townhouse, was he not? So why did none of your staff see him leave with it?"

Phillip blew out a breath of frustration, feeling as if they were coming up with more questions than answers. "And even in this, it might well be that he is not at all responsible and we have made an error in judgment," he said, scowling. "But what else can we do but seek out the truth?"

"The truth must always be uncovered," Lady Rosalyn said, a sweetness in her tone which set a fire in Phillip's heart again, "for it can change so many things, can it not?"

"Indeed," Phillip answered, giving her a long look and praying that, very soon, they would both be able to speak in private again. "And in this – as in so many other things – I am determined to find it."

15

Rosalyn tilted her head, looking at one of the paintings on the wall next to the space where the missing painting ought to be. She had never truly appreciated art, and thus, these meant very little to her. Yes, she could admire their beauty, but she could not tell one artist's stroke from another. Nor could she understand the desire to have one particular artwork. To her, they were all very nice and some very beautiful, but she did not have any great sense of passion for them.

"You are not thinking of stealing one of these paintings, are you?"

A light shiver ran over her skin as she turned to look up at Lord Waverley. "No, I was not thinking of it." Aware that they had only very recently almost stepped forward into a new part of their connection, Rosalyn gently touched his hand. "We have a conversation to finish, do we not?"

A light flush touched Lord Waverley's throat, rising up quickly into his face. "You are bolder than I, Rosalyn."

A sudden concern lurched in her throat, and she made to step back, only for him to catch her hand tightly.

"I meant only that I wanted very much to speak with you about these things, but thus far, I have not found the right words. It has been three days since that conversation, and I have said nothing!" A glimmer of frustration flashed in his eyes, his lips thinning for a moment as he looked away, only to press her hand again. "Rosalyn, I want *very* much to speak with you, for there is a good deal more for me to say. Though how can we do so when there is always someone present?"

Hearing voices approaching the hallway, Rosalyn sighed and took her hand from his. "Mayhap, once we have determined the truth about the painting, we will be able to speak. My brother might... " Trailing off, a frown tugged at her forehead as she remembered one or two things that her brother had said to her previously, things that had not made sense. Could it be that he had recognized what was in her heart for Lord Waverley before she had done?

"Rosalyn?"

A sudden, bright smile touched her lips as she looked back up at him. "I am sure that, should I ask my brother, he will give us a few minutes to speak alone. In fact, I think he might even encourage it!"

There was no time for her to give him any further explanation, for the other bluestocking soon came into the hallway, followed by her brother and Lord Albury. They were all to gather together to discuss the matter of the painting and to ascertain how Lord Coates – or whoever the guilty party was – had removed the painting from the house. It was late in the evening, but the other bluestockings had been permitted to come since the occasion was only a small gathering of familiar friends, for which Rosalyn was grateful. She needed them all here this evening. The mystery *had* to be solved.

"So, shall we begin?" she asked, as her friends drew near. "Lord Waverley, as we know, was in the kitchen and then waylaid by someone who took him to the library. If we go to where the other gentlemen were, then mayhap my brother or Lord Waverley might remember another detail, or we will be able to ascertain when the painting itself might have been taken."

"And how it was taken out of the house," Lord Waverley added, as the other bluestockings nodded. "This way, if you please."

He led them towards the drawing room, pointing to where the dining room was also.

"Shall you and I be Lord Whittaker and Lord Raleigh, my love?" Lord Albury asked, grinning broadly at Miss Trentworth. "We must be in the dining room, yes?"

Miss Trentworth laughed and put her hand on his arm. "Yes, we must."

"Though might you stay by the door?" Rosalyn asked, seeing Miss Trentworth's look of love towards her betrothed. "Not because I do not trust you, but because we all must be able to talk to each other about what might have happened next."

With a nod and a smile, Miss Trentworth and Lord Albury moved away from the group towards the dining room. With a deep breath, Rosalyn looked back at the rest of the bluestockings. "Fairchild, you were present here, yes?"

"Yes, with Lord Coates and Lord Haverstock. And Lord Stockton was in the hallway," her brother confirmed. "That, I do recall."

"And Lord Mansfield was also present, about to take his leave," Lady Isobella interjected. "Is that not so?"

With another word of confirmation, Lady Isobella came to stand in the hallway, pretending to be Lord Stockton.

Lady Amelia, Lord Fairchild, and Miss Sherwood walked into the drawing room but stood near the door.

"And I was absent," Lord Waverley muttered, rubbing one hand over his eyes. "Lord Mansfield was present and – "

"Then I shall be Lord Mansfield." Walking into the drawing room, she smiled at her brother. "Fairchild, might you sit where you were on that evening? And direct Lady Amelia and Miss Sherwood as to where the other two gentlemen were?" Once they had done so, Rosalyn came herself a little further into the room. "Lord Mansfield was present also, yes?"

Her brother nodded. "Yes, he stood in front of the mantlepiece to take his farewell."

Rosalyn walked to stand in that very place. "I come to bid you farewell, but before I am finished, Lord Stockton comes staggering into the room." On cue, Lady Isobella stepped in, nodding to Lord Fairchild. "He says he has – "

"He says he has dropped the decanter and does not know what to do," her brother interrupted, though Rosalyn did not think he had meant to, given the slightly narrowed look about his eyes. Clearly, he was doing his best to remember everything that had taken place. "Lord Coates was nearest to him." He pointed to Lady Amelia. "And he begged for his help. Lord Coates rolled his eyes but got to his feet."

Lady Amelia rose. "If I must help you, then I shall," she said as though she truly was Lord Coates, following Lady Isobella from the room.

"Then it was only yourself, Lord Mansfield, and Lord Haverstock." Rosalyn looked keenly at her brother, who nodded. "Then what happened?"

With a scowl, Lord Fairchild shook his head. "I do not

recall exactly. Lord Mansfield took his leave thereafter, of that, I am sure."

Rosalyn walked to the door but did not go through it. "And he saw Lord Coates and Lord Stockton, I presume."

Lord Waverley shrugged. "Mayhap. I was not present, so I cannot be sure. We could ask the butler to confirm."

She nodded. "Let us presume that Lord Mansfield walked past Lord Coates and Lord Stockton in the hallway, along with the butler who came to their aid. He quit the room, leaving only yourself, Fairchild, and Lord Haverstock in here alone."

Her brother snorted. "Lord Haverstock was no good for conversation, I remember that. The moment he sat down, his eyes closed and he fell asleep!"

Rosalyn's eyebrows lifted. "You remember that?"

"I... I do." He blinked, then frowned. "I was hopeful for some better conversation, but Lord Stockton was much too in his cups! At that juncture, I decided to pour another drink for myself and... well, the rest is nothing more than a blur."

Considering this, Rosalyn frowned, the quietness in the room helped her think. Thinking quickly, she tried to close her eyes and thought about where everyone was the moment Lord Mansfield had quit the room, only for her eyes to fly open as a breath caught in her throat.

Lord Waverley was beside her at once. "What? What is it?"

"Lord Coates." Hurrying forward, Rosalyn looked straight into her brother's eyes. "You did not mention Lord Coates. You said only that Lord Haverstock and Lord Stockton were not good company, for Lord Haverstock fell asleep, and Lord Stockton was too overcome with liquor. So what of Lord Coates?"

Her brother frowned. "I – I do not recall."

Rosalyn's heart slammed hard against her ribs. "Does this mean, then, that when Lord Coates quit the room to help Lord Stockton, he did not immediately return?"

"He must have returned at some point, however," Lady Isobella said, coming to join her in the center of the drawing room. "That was where the staff found him."

"So, therefore, if he *did* steal the painting, then it was removed from the house by his hands before he returned to join the other guests." Rosalyn looked to Lord Waverley, seeing his eyes flare wide. "Is that not so?"

"But how would that be possible?" Miss Trentworth and Lord Albury came into the room to join them, clearly overhearing the last that Rosalyn had said. "You told us that the butler said the footmen and maids and he were to and fro in the house, cleaning the floor and picking up after the decanter and glass."

The room fell silent again as everyone in the room thought hard. Rosalyn glanced up towards Lord Waverley, seeing his frown and the way his eyes lingered on the floor at his feet.

"Unless," she said, slowly, the idea coming to her seeming so foolish and preposterous. "Unless he did not remove the painting from the house, choosing to leave it here for another time?"

Every head turned to her, and Rosalyn ducked hers, embarrassment clutching at her. Perhaps she ought not to have given voice to what she had thought. Mayhap it was much too ridiculous for words.

"It would explain, I suppose, why none from your staff saw the painting being taken." Lord Albury nodded in Rosalyn's direction. "If you are right, Lady Rosalyn, then he has hidden the painting somewhere very strange and will now be thinking of a way to steal it from you a second time!"

"It is an ingenious plan, if it is what has happened," Miss Sherwood agreed, her eyes a little wider than usual. "Would he truly have done such a thing? And for what purpose?"

"*That* is the trouble," Lord Waverley admitted, spreading out his hands. "I cannot understand the reasoning behind such a thought. Though," he continued, dropping his hands back to his sides, "if he has been speaking to Lord Hemmingway and Lord Pentland, then there must be a purpose behind it."

"And he did appear to be upset during that conversation," Rosalyn added, as Lord Waverley nodded slowly. "Mayhap they want to know where the painting is, and he is not yet ready to give it to them."

"Mayhap." Lord Waverley smiled briefly, but it did not light his eyes. "Then should we search the house, do you think? Try to find the painting?"

Rosalyn smiled back at him. "The library might be a good place to look. Lord Coates, for it does appear to be him, had you in the library for a purpose."

Lord Fairchild got to his feet. "To give you the brandy with the drug in it."

"*And* mayhap to hide the painting." Rosalyn looked all around her friends as they clustered together. "But if we do not find it, then what do we do?"

It took only a second for her brother to respond, a dark smile shooting shadows up into his eyes. "Then you throw another occasion, Lord Waverley. You throw a soiree and we are all invited – Lord Coates, Lord Hemmingway, and Lord Pentland too."

Pulling to the idea, Rosalyn nodded fervently. "Indeed, even if the painting *is* found, you could set someone to guard the place, to make sure that Lord Coates returns for it, catching him that way. Otherwise, we must all pay close attention to the fellow when he attends. We must hope that he will either reveal the location of the painting or, instead, tell us of his connection to Lord Hemmingway and Lord Pentland."

Rosalyn's stomach twisted. "There is still a chance it was not he who took it," she said, speaking softly. "But the evidence is beginning to collect itself together and points towards Lord Coates."

"It does," Miss Sherwood agreed. "And now all we must do is uncover the truth. We are getting closer." She smiled and encouragement lifted Rosalyn's heart. "I can feel it."

16

"What is the meaning of this?"

Phillip came to a stop, trying to hide his exasperation as both Lord Hemmingway and Lord Pentland came to stand directly in his path. "Good afternoon, gentlemen."

"What is the meaning of this?" Lord Pentland said again, pointing one finger at Phillip's chest and coming dangerously close to prodding him. "Why would you invite us to your soiree? What is it that you intend for us?"

Phillip lifted his eyebrows in feigned surprise. Sending the invitations to Lord Hemmingway and Lord Pentland had been difficult to do, but he had known it was of the greatest importance. Whatever they had been discussing with Lord Coates, it was his hope and expectation that it would all cumulate at his soiree, and Phillip wanted to discover the truth in its entirety, even if it did not involve his painting.

"You do not care for either of us, you have made that *very* clear," Lord Hemmingway stated, his eyes flashing. "And yet you invite us to your soiree? There is something more to this, I am sure."

Lifting his chin and standing as tall as he could, Phillip held each gentleman's gaze for a few seconds before he responded. "I would have thought an invitation would have been appreciated rather than complained about."

This made both Lord Hemmingway and Lord Pentland narrow their eyes at him, still clearly quite determined to find out the truth – a truth that Phillip was not willing to give.

"You have stated that I am just as my father was," Phillip continued when they said nothing, but neither did they refuse to move out of his way. "However, I have proven, time and again that I am not like he was. Therefore, when I invite the gentlemen who dislike me to my soiree, I am doing just the opposite of what he would have done, am I not?"

Lord Hemmingway exchanged a glance with his friend, then looked back at Phillip. "You are telling me that the only reason for your invitation is to show us that you are not what we think of you?"

Phillip nodded. "Precisely." The truth was not something he intended to share with them both, and mayhap they would not come to his soiree, but he had to try. "I do not hold grudges. I do not treat members of the *ton* as though they are enemies. If you choose to be cruel and to lie about me, then I shall not respond in kind. *That* was precisely what my father would have done, and, as I have said already, many a time, I have no intention of behaving in any way like him."

This did not seem to sit well with Lord Hemmingway and Lord Pentland for they both shared another uneasy glance, with Lord Hemmingway shuffling his feet and Lord Pentland looking down at the ground.

"I must take my leave of you both," Phillip stated, hoping that his strong stance would be enough to have them do as he asked. "If you would not mind stepping out of my path?" Keeping his gaze centered on Lord Pentland, he set his shoulders back and kept his head lifted. Much to his relief, after a few seconds, they moved themselves out of his way and, heads close together, walked in the opposite direction from Phillip, clearly discussing all that Phillip had told them. Relief billowing in his chest, Phillip carried on his way, only for another familiar gentleman to join him.

"My friend!"

Phillip tried to smile, hoping he appeared nonchalant as Lord Coates greeted him warmly. "Good afternoon, Lord Coates."

"Whatever were you doing talking to Lord Hemmingway and Lord Pentland?" the gentleman glanced, casting a dark glance over his shoulder in their direction. "Were they seeking to upset you again in some way? Mayhap they are frustrated at how the *ton* has slowly begun to turn back towards you."

Phillip shrugged his shoulders. "They are confused as to why I invited them to my soiree."

Lord Coates came to a sudden and unexpected stop, making Phillip turn to look at him. "You – you invited them?"

"I did," Phillip noted Lord Coates' astonished reaction but feigned a smile of nonchalance. "They are determined to believe me akin to my father in every way, and is this not a way to show them that I am quite the opposite? Though, I have very little hope that they will attend."

"Of course." Lord Coates' smile returned, though it did not have as much strength as before. "I have responded to your invitation already and we – my wife, my daughter, and I – will be delighted to join you." He began to walk alongside Phillip again. "Indeed, I am very glad indeed to know that you are not about to permit the *ton* to push you back into shadow."

"Thank you." Phillip glanced at the jovial gentleman, wondering how it could be that a gentleman such as he could have stolen from him. *If* it was Lord Coates at all. "I did fear that speaking aloud as I did at the soiree would have sent yet more of the *ton* from me, but it appears to have done the opposite!"

"Indeed it has!" Lord Coates beamed at him, all trace of confusion and surprise gone. "I am glad for you, truly. Now, where are you going this fine day? Are you thinking about Gunters? It is in this direction, is it not?"

Phillip smiled again but felt his heart sink lower, disliking the feeling that Lord Coates was putting on nothing more than a façade for him at the present moment. "I am going to the bookshop, in fact. Lady Rosalyn and Lord Fairchild thought to take a turn about the shops this afternoon, and I said I would join them."

Lord Coates' smile wavered. "Lord Fairchild is near?"

"Yes, he is." A little confused by the gentleman's sudden change of demeanor, Phillip frowned. "Is there something wrong?"

The smile quickly stretched wide again. "No, no, not in the least. It is only that my daughter... " Letting his sentence stutter to a close, he shrugged and looked away. "I should take my leave of you. I am to go to Gunters myself, for my daughter and wife are enjoying an ice at this very moment!"

"Then I hope you partake of one also," Phillip answered, watching the gentleman walk away. "Good afternoon." A heaviness settled on his heart as he walked to the bookshop, quite certain that this was where he would find Lady Rosalyn and her brother. After their conversation at his townhouse the previous afternoon, Phillip had so many considerations on his mind, it had been difficult to think of anything else! At the same time, though he admitted to himself that the unfinished conversation between himself and Lady Rosalyn was just as much of a burden upon him as the missing painting, if not more so! Thus, in hearing that they were both to step out into the heart of London this afternoon, Phillip had taken the opportunity held out to him and decided to come in search of them. Mayhap, that way, he would be able to steal Lady Rosalyn away for even a few minutes and could talk about all that was now on his heart.

Pushing open the door to the bookshop, he stepped inside and looked around. A broad grin spread right across his face as he spotted Lord Fairchild standing to his right, a book in his hand, but his gaze fixed to the window and all that went on outside. Chuckling to himself, Phillip came a little closer and tapped his friend on the shoulder.

"I think you have to look at the book if you want to read it."

Lord Fairchild started in surprise, then grunted back at him, rolling his eyes. "I *am* trying to read. I was only thinking about whether or not this book would be suitable."

"Is that so?" With another chuckle, Phillip shook his head. "My friend, you have as much on your mind as I do. Though mayhap, that comes from different sources." When Lord Fairchild lifted his eyebrows in question, Phillip spread out his hands. "I was speaking to Lord Coates only a few moments ago."

"Lord Coates?" Instantly, the book was forgotten as Lord Fairchild's eyes rounded. "What did he say? Was there any mention of the painting?"

Phillip shook his head no. "The only thing he spoke of was his daughter. She is at Gunters with her mother." He let a beat of silence fall before he continued. "Pray do not tell me that your attentions to her have ceased because of what her father might have done?"

With a hiss of breath escaping him, Lord Fairchild dropped his gaze. "It is not as simple as you make out, my friend. Yes, I will admit that I think very highly of Lady Catherine and have, yes, been interested in her company – but that is all it can be! I cannot let myself be at all close to her, for her father might be... well, a thief."

"But that does not mean you ought to pull yourself away from her, does it?" Phillip asked, surprised at not only his friend's words but his own, fierce reaction. "My father was a despicable fellow. Would you keep Rosalyn from my company because of his actions?"

Lord Fairchild opened his mouth to say no, only to scowl and turn his head away.

"You see my point, I think."

"You are a little *too* on point." Lord Fairchild sighed and pinched the bridge of his nose. "Truth be told, I am not at all certain about anything. I did not ever think that I would find myself in a situation where my heart was doing all manner of strange things!"

"Our hearts have a way of surprising us," Phillip answered, resisting the urge to turn his head and look for Rosalyn. "In light of that, Fairchild, I must – well, I must be honest with you about all that I am feeling at present."

This sent a broad smile across Lord Fairchild's face, surprising Phillip with such a reaction.

"You appear... pleased."

"This is about Rosalyn, is it not?" Lord Fairchild threw his head back and laughed as Phillip flushed hot, the sound echoing through the bookshop. Phillip looked at the floor, his shoulders hunched as he prayed for the floor to open up and swallow him whole, such was the attention that Lord Fairchild was drawing to them both. He could only hope that there were no others around them who had heard Lord Fairchild speak Rosalyn's name.

"You do not need to look so embarrassed!" Lord Fairchild exclaimed, clapping Phillip on the arm, his grin still fixed. "I have been *waiting* for this moment for a very long time indeed. Actually, I have been wondering what has been taking both of you so very long to admit all that you feel, worrying that I would have to intervene in some way."

Phillip glanced all around him, keeping his voice low. "Please, my friend. If you would not mind declaring to all the others present just how much you have known before me, then I would be grateful."

This made the grin soften just a little.

"I thank you."

"You are welcome." Lord Fairchild chuckled, showing not even the smallest bit of remorse over his loud declarations. "What *has* taken you so long, Waverley? Was it just that you did not know what to do with your affection?"

Phillip hesitated then, seeing no reason for him to hide the truth, and spread out his hands. "I found myself in the very same position as you are now, albeit in a slightly different manner."

"What do you mean?"

Glancing over his shoulder to make sure Lady Rosalyn was nowhere near them, Phillip took a small step closer to his friend, determined to speak quietly. "I have long thought of Rosalyn in affectionate terms, Fairchild. But my father's behavior meant that I would not permit myself to think of her as anything more than that."

Lord Fairchild's smile was gone completely now.

"When he died, you might well think I would feel myself

able to pursue her again," Phillip continued, with a wry smile. "But I could not. Coming to London and seeing just how the *ton* viewed me was severe indeed, and I felt the weight of it sitting heavily upon my shoulders."

"I see." Lord Fairchild ran a hand over his chin, his eyes thoughtful. "Your care for her was so great; you did not want to injure her by coming close to her."

"Precisely." Phillip sighed heavily. "The truth is, I wanted to protect her from all that the *ton* said of me. I was afraid that, if I told her how I felt and if, by any luck, she had even the smallest of affection for me, my reputation would besmirch her. I could not do that to her."

Lord Fairchild set a hand on Phillip's shoulder, looking straight back at him. "Rosalyn would not have cared about that, my friend. Neither would I."

"I know that. But my heart cared so much for her, it would not let me do such a thing. I felt myself unworthy of her, Fairchild. In many ways, I still do."

Lord Fairchild's hand fell back to his side, though his gaze remained steady. "There is nothing that separates you."

A small smile touched Phillip's lips as he thought of the lady he loved. "She is gentleness, beauty, kindness, wisdom, and more. I am in her shadow in almost everything. Besides, I do not have a great fortune any longer, though I am taking great pains to improve it."

"Again," Lord Fairchild said, steadily, "that does not matter one jot. Rosalyn would be deeply upset with both me and you if she were ever to hear that your lack of abundance was a reason to keep you from her."

Hope flared hot in Phillip's heart. "Then might I ask – and I ask this in great humbleness – whether you might permit me to ask Rosalyn for her hand?"

Lord Fairchild did not grin, did not laugh aloud as

Phillip had expected. Instead, he only smiled gently and nodded, making an explosion of relief tear through Phillip's frame.

"I thank you." Putting one hand to his heart, he inclined his head. "I am grateful, Fairchild. Do you think...?" Frowning, he glanced over his shoulder again, but she was still nowhere to be seen. "Do you think she will say yes?"

A shout of laughter from Lord Fairchild made Phillip flush hot, a self-conscious smile brushing his lips.

"Given what I very nearly stumbled upon when I came to find her at your townhouse some days ago, I have every expectation that she will throw herself willingly into your arms," Lord Fairchild said, a brightness in his expression that Phillip had never before seen, not in all their years of friendship. "She may have only just begun to realize it, Waverley, but my sister has cared for you for many a year." He smiled when Phillip's eyebrows rose. "All you need do now is ask her."

17

"Are you as anxious as I?"

Rosalyn smiled quickly, aware of the butterflies that poured into her stomach. "Yes, Eugenia, I am." The soiree was well underway, but all the bluestockings, herself included, were spread through the house. The search for the painting had been fruitless, which meant that their only hope now was for someone – either Lord Coates or someone else – to lead them to it.

"The parlor is empty," Miss Sherwood said, glancing towards it as they lingered by the door of the library. "The entertainment is soon to begin, is it not?"

"Yes, very soon," Rosalyn answered, clasping her hands tightly together in an effort to remove some of the anxiety from her frame. "The guests will come to the drawing room for the entertainment – a play of some description, I believe. There will be a short intermission between the first half and the second, so in that time, they will be ushered to the dining room so they might have some refreshment."

"That way, the dining room will first be empty of guests, as well as the other rooms of the house, and then the drawing room." Miss Sherwood pressed her lips flat. "Are you quite ready to hide yourself away?"

Rosalyn nodded, only for Lord Waverley to appear, coming quickly towards them. His eyes were bright with, Rosalyn presumed, the same mixture of anticipation and worry that she felt.

"I am about to have the guests come to the drawing-room," he said quietly. "Are you quite ready?"

Rosalyn nodded. "I am." Miss Sherwood was to sit with the other guests in the drawing room, as was Miss Trentworth. They would sit at the back of the room to see if anyone took their leave and, thereafter, would linger in the drawing room in case anyone returned. Lady Amelia, Lady Isobella, and Rosalyn herself were to stand in various parts of the house, hiding themselves from sight in the hope that someone, somewhere, would do something and reveal the painting to them.

"Then I shall go," Lord Waverley said, looking down into Rosalyn's eyes. "If only I did not have to be seen by my guests, I would do all that I could to help!"

"I have my brother," Rosalyn reminded him. "He will be nearby."

With a nod, Lord Waverley made to reach out to her, only for his gaze to slide to Miss Sherwood and his hand to drop back to his side. With a small smile, he turned away, leaving Rosalyn to watch after him, her heart aching suddenly.

"He is still to profess his love for you, then?" Miss Sherwood's smile was light, her voice teasing, but the truth still held there. "You will return his words of love, I am sure."

Rosalyn let out a slow breath, aware that the butterflies in her stomach had increased twofold thanks to Lord Waverley's presence. "I must keep my mind on this at present," she said, not answering her friend's question. "But yes, nothing has been said as yet."

Miss Sherwood took her hand, pressed it, and then stepped away. "It will be over soon, I am sure," she said, before taking her leave. Rosalyn watched her depart, her heart quickening all the more as she stepped back into a small alcove, hiding herself away. She could hear the other guests taking their leave of their present conversation and going to the drawing room, ready to be swept away in delight by the play whilst she remained exactly where she was. The quietness that followed made her feel all the more anxious, her fingers gripping tightly together as she closed her eyes and steadied her breathing.

This was the moment when the mystery could be solved, when the culprit could be revealed and the entire story could come to its unhappy conclusion... and yet, there was no promise that it would be so. There was no hope that this soiree would do as they intended.

Quite how long she stood there for, Rosalyn did not know. It felt like hours, though Lord Waverley had promised her it would not be for too long that the play went on. She had half expected someone – namely, Lord Coates – to run from the play and do what he must, but there came no presence near her, no footsteps to indicate anyone else nearby. Sighing to herself, Rosalyn leaned back and closed her eyes, her worry slowly dissipating.

Eventually, the sound of raucous laughter and loud conversation reached her ears. Peeking out carefully, she saw the guests moving from the drawing room to the dining room. The first part of the play was at an end, then. Moving back into the shadows of the alcove as best she could, Rosalyn closed her eyes again, focusing on breathing at a slow and steady pace.

He is still to profess his love for you, then? Miss Sherwood's voice came back to her ears almost as if she were standing beside her. Rosalyn did not open her eyes, letting the edges of her lips curve. No, he had not yet said anything, and indeed, neither had she, but the intention for them to do so was there. He had made that clear enough, and Rosalyn could hardly wait for that moment to take place. She wanted desperately to be able to tell him what she had discovered in her heart for him, wanted to acknowledge that all she had felt for him was, in fact, a good deal more than one would feel for a brother! What would he do when she told him such things? Would he capture her in his arms, as she so desperately hoped he might? Would he lower his head to kiss her? Rosalyn had never been kissed before, and even the thought was both terrifying and wonderful in equal measure.

A sudden sound made her eyes open wide, her breath hitching in her chest as gentle footfalls caught her attention. She swallowed tightly, pressing her back against the wall of the alcove and doing her best to stand quietly and move not an inch. The footsteps were coming closer now, leaving her in no doubt that someone was approaching. Holding her breath, she waited for the person to pass, her eyes begging her to close them as though, somehow, that would shut out the sight of her from whoever it was.

The footsteps came closer, and Rosalyn's skin crawled, only for them to pass her without hesitation. Letting out a slow, steady breath, she opened her eyes and loosened her hands, tension beginning to crawl up her spine and into her chest once more.

Who is it?

The gentleman ahead of her had dark hair and broad shoulders but, then again, so did many a gentleman. When he paused, she pulled herself quickly back into the alcove, praying that he did not see her as he turned his head to look over his shoulder.

Lord Coates!

Her heart pounded as she paused, seeing him step into the library. What ought she to do? Go after him or go in search of Lord Waverley?

Coming slowly out of the alcove, she looked all around, seeing a footman passing a short distance away. On slippered feet that made no sound, she hurried to him, demanding, in hushed tones, that Lord Waverley come to the library at once, only to turn on her heel and hurry back towards the library itself.

The door was ajar, and Rosalyn pushed herself close to the door, trying to look through it rather than step inside without hesitation. She could see nothing, only a few shadows here and there from the candlelight. Closing her eyes, she tried to quieten the pounding of her heart before, with courage like a thread slipping from her fingers, she stepped into the library.

The door itself did not creak as Rosalyn pushed it a little further open, fervently hoping that Lord Waverley would soon come to join her so she did not have to face this gentleman alone. Her first thought was that there was no one present, that the gentleman had gone into a different room when she had gone to speak with the footman. Frowning, she took another step inside, only for her to start at a scraping sound that seemed to come from near the fireplace.

Stumbling back, she held her breath, her hands clutched together at her chest, and her back pressed against one of the bookcases as something in the room moved. Her eyes flared wide as she saw the bookshelf nearest to the fireplace begin to swing towards her, forcing her, on trembling legs, to hurry to the corner of the room so she might cover herself in shadow.

A door?

It was not unusual for houses of this magnitude to have secret passageways and the like, but Lord Waverley had never mentioned it to her – nor any of them when they had come to search the house. Could it be that he did not know of it? And if that were so, then how did Lord Coates know of its presence?

"Do you have it?"

Much to Rosalyn's astonishment, it was not Lord Waverley who came into the room, as she had anticipated, but Lord Hemmingway. He strode into the library as though he were the master of the house who had every right to be present, shutting the door behind him and not so much as glancing towards the corner where Rosalyn stood.

"I have it." Lord Coates emerged from the open door, a cloth-covered object in his hands. "Though you know that I have no desire to do this, Hemmingway. Lord Waverley is – "

"I care nothing for what it is you want," Lord Coates stated dismissively. "Now, do hurry up. The other half of the play will soon begin, and I shall take my leave then. *With* the painting."

Lord Coates turned, closed the door, and then, with a grimace, came back towards Lord Hemmingway. "This displeases me a great deal. Lord Waverley is someone I consider to be a friend."

"I care not." Reaching out, Lord Hemmingway took the painting from Lord Coates as Rosalyn looked on, trying to understand all that was taking place. "I shall take my leave of the house in a few minutes, once the guests have been called to the drawing room. You shall have to make your way there also, Lord Coates, for the *ton* will expect to see you."

Lord Coates scowled. "Whereas they will think nothing of you leaving halfway through a society event, no?" With Lord Hemmingway grinning darkly at this remark, Lord Coates sighed heavily and ran a hand over his forehead. "Do you now consider my debts paid?"

Lord Hemmingway sniffed and tilted his head. "I suppose that I might. Though there is also the matter of interest."

"Interest?" Lord Coates threw up his hands. "That is not something you mentioned to me before!"

"You have owed me a significant amount of coin for near a year, Lord Coates!" Lord Hemmingway exclaimed, making Rosalyn wince where she stood at the anger and upset in the gentleman's voice. "Then you choose to spend it on your daughter!"

"She is to have her Season!" Lord Coates exclaimed. "I could not reject her for that, not on my account. It is my fault that the debts came to me in the first place! But I will not turn my back upon my daughter. I will give her what *she* is owed, just as I have now done my duty to you."

Lord Hemmingway laughed, but the sound was cruel, filled with evil, and making Rosalyn tremble. Just where was Lord Waverley?

"*I* shall decide whether or not your debt has been repaid in full, Lord Coates! Do not think for a *moment* that you have any say in this!"

"But... but you promised," Lord Coates answered feebly. "You told me that – "

"Just what did he tell you?"

Sagging a little from relief, Rosalyn stayed where she was in the corner of the room as not only Lord Waverley but her brother strode into the room, with her brother staying by the door so that the two gentlemen could not leave.

"Lord – Lord Waverley." Lord Coates immediately began to stammer, his eyes darting from Lord Waverley to Lord Hemmingway and back again. "I – I am terribly sorry, but I –"

"Lord Waverley, I have just now discovered Lord Coates making his way from your house with *this*." Lord Hemmingway thrust the painting into Lord Waverley's hands, throwing a disparaging look towards Lord Coates. "I cannot tell what it is but I presume it belongs to this house?"

"That is not - !"

Lord Hemmingway sliced the air between himself and Lord Coates. "*Might* I suggest, Lord Coates, that you say nothing? After all, what you have done thus far is worthy of great punishment, and I do not know how you shall *ever* repay such a debt."

Rosalyn, who had still not revealed herself, watched as Lord Coates opened his mouth and then closed it again, his shoulders rounding as his head lowered. Clearly, he understood what Lord Hemmingway was saying, just as Rosalyn did. If he spoke the truth and said that Lord Hemmingway had been the one seeking this painting, then the debts upon him would only increase. If he stayed silent and took the blame, then mayhap Lord Hemmingway would do nothing more. His financial debt would be considered fulfilled, whilst the disgrace he would bear would linger long.

Anger built like a furnace in Rosalyn's chest, seeing how defeated Lord Coates appeared. Yes, what he had done was wrong in itself, but to be forced to take the blame for it all too much. Lord Hemmingway was responsible for it all, *not* Lord Coates.

"Is that so?" Lord Waverley, much to her relief, did not sound convinced, though Lord Hemmingway was nodding fervently. "Then, I presume you wish for me to thank you for what you have done in stopping him, Lord Hemmingway? Though I admit to being a little surprised to see you here, given that the other guests were in the dining room and are only now making their way to the drawing room."

Lord Hemmingway drew himself up. "I saw Lord Coates come to the library," he said in a commanding tone. "Intrigued, I followed after him. That is when I saw him with this painting."

"Is that true, Lord Coates?" Lord Waverley's voice had grown hard, and Rosalyn, hearing it, took her first step out of the shadows. "Is this all true?"

Lord Coates dropped his head forward, his shoulders rounded. "I took the painting from your wall on the night of the soiree," he admitted, as Rosalyn took another few steps closer. No gentleman had noticed her as yet, though she hoped Lord Waverley knew of her presence here. "I hid it in the hope of retrieving it at another opportune time."

"And why did you try to steal it?" Lord Fairchild wanted to know from his position by the door. "What purpose did you have in taking it?"

Lord Coates opened and then closed his mouth, a frown on his forehead. The way he looked to Lord Hemmingway for aid told Rosalyn everything she needed to know.

"You needed only to ask for the price," Lord Waverley said, his voice quiet. "I would have given it to you if you had asked. It does not mean a great deal to me."

Lord Coates' only answer was to hang his head.

"Well, I am glad to have been able to return it," Lord Hemmingway said in a cheerful tone. "I shall return, with the other guests, to your most *excellent* entertainment, Lord Waverley. I am glad that we have been able to set previous... upsets behind us. Do excuse me."

"Wait a moment, if you please." Rosalyn, taking quicker steps now, came to stand directly beside Lord Waverley, facing Lord Hemmingway, who upon seeing her, stumbled back in shock.

"I did hope you were here," Lord Waverley murmured, setting the painting down and slipping one hand around her waist for only a moment. "You heard everything, I assume?"

"I did." Rosalyn lifted her chin, confidence filling her as she looked directly into Lord Hemmingway's face. "Goodness, Lord Hemmingway, you are an exceedingly good liar, are you not? It is a shame that such a quality is not well thought of, else you would have exceeded us all in good standing!"

Lord Hemmingway's face had paled, but as she held his gaze, he stood straight and pulled his shoulders back, perhaps trying desperately to preserve himself somehow. "I do not know what you mean."

"Yes, you do," she said, looking now to Lord Coates. "My dear Lord Coates, you are in a difficult situation, are you not?" When he said nothing, she took a small step closer to him, sympathy pushing through to her heart. "I heard every word that was said," she continued, his gaze flicking to hers and then going to Lord Hemmingway. "You need not be afraid of him. I heard everything, Lord Coates, and I can assure you that taking the blame when it is Lord Hemmingway at fault will do you no good."

"The shame ought to be his," Lord Waverley said firmly. "Do not bear a burden you ought not to carry, my friend. Tell me the truth and I shall do all I can to help you."

Lord Coates hesitated for only a few more seconds before, with a huge exhale of breath, he dropped his head and rubbed both hands over his face. "I am sorry."

"I know you did not want to do this," Rosalyn said, gently, not looking towards Lord Hemmingway any longer. "You owe a debt to Lord Hemmingway?"

Lord Coates let out a low groan rather than saying anything in response.

"And he demanded you steal this painting from Lord Waverley?" Rosalyn continued, taking another step towards the gentleman. "That way, your debt would be repaid?"

"I thought it would take that weight from me." Lord Coates finally spoke, lifting his head and looking back at her with wide, frightened eyes. "But as you heard, it has done nothing but make me even more of a fool than I was before."

She smiled gently, putting one hand out on his shoulder. "You are no fool," she promised, softly. "Now, tell Lord Waverley everything. As he has said so many times, he is not his father and he will not treat you cruelly." Turning her head, she looked into the eyes of the gentleman she loved and felt her heart fill with a fresh affection for him as he returned her smile. "He will understand. I promise you that."

18

"Lady Rosalyn speaks very highly of me, but in this case, she speaks the truth." Phillip, whose heart had not stopped thundering wildly in his chest since the footman had come to find him, pulled his gaze from Lady Rosalyn. He looked at Lord Coates, who had something of a terrified expression on his face. "And Lord Hemmingway, do not think for a moment that I cannot see you trying to skulk towards the door." Turning his whole body towards the guilty gentleman, he gestured towards the door. "You are aware that Lord Fairchild is present, are you not? He is standing by the door so you cannot escape. And, even if you were to force your way past him, I have Lord Albury also waiting outside. So you see? You can go nowhere."

This made Lord Hemmingway's face pale all the more, making him appear almost ghostlike in the candlelight. With a nod and a grim smile towards Lord Fairchild, Phillip returned his attention to Lord Coates, who, seemingly weak from what had just occurred, had now sank into a chair, his head in his hands. Lady Rosalyn was sitting near him, concern shining in her eyes as she looked back towards Phillip. How proud he was of her for all she had done! She had not only sent the footman for him, she had, thereafter, hidden herself away in the library – at great risk to herself – and had overheard all that had taken place. Had she not done such a thing, then Lord Coates might, at this very moment, be taking the blame for something he had not done, and Lord Hemmingway would be smiling to himself at his cleverness.

He did not want to think what might have happened had she been discovered eavesdropping on Lord Hemmingway's plan.

"Tell me, Lord Coates." Refocusing his thoughts, Phillip made his way towards the gentleman but sat down opposite so he would not be towering over him. "What did Lord Hemmingway have you do?"

Lord Coates did not lift his head. "Lord Hemmingway despises you, Lord Waverley." He spoke without intonation, his voice flat and heavy. "I was directed to steal a painting from your house."

"Why?"

With a long exhale of breath, Lord Coates finally lifted his head and looked back at Phillip. "It came up in conversation." He paused, then began to explain himself as Lord Hemmingway hovered in the background. "I am a fool, Lord Waverley." Eyes closed, he groaned aloud again, as if what he was to say was nothing was a heavy burden upon him. "My interest in gambling is much too severe. I have lost a great deal although I have regained some."

"And you owed a gambling debt," Phillip said, slowly. "To Lord Hemmingway."

"One that I could not repay. And when I *did* have the coin, I chose instead to spend it on my daughter's Season so that she might be successful." Lord Coates' voice broke. "I am not in the least bit regretful that I made that choice. It was the right thing to do."

"Lady Catherine will be grateful for your choice to put her before Lord Hemmingway," Lady Rosalyn said, gently as Phillip watched her lean across to put a hand on Lord Coates' arm. "You ought not to feel any guilt in that."

With a small sniff, Lord Coates nodded though he did not lift his head.

"So you spoke of the painting?" Phillip asked as Lord Coates nodded. "When?"

"After your dinner," Lord Coates said, dully. "Lord Hemmingway was asking why I was associating with you, reminding me of how much he despised you, and thus, I stated that I had enjoyed the dinner and the discussion about your painting."

Phillip turned his head to see Lord Hemmingway close his eyes as if frustrated and angry that Lord Coates had said something.

"And you thought to steal my painting?" Phillip asked, moving away from Lord Coates and towards Lord Hemmingway. "You thought that stealing my painting would settle Lord Coates' debt in some way?"

Lord Hemmingway said nothing though he did open his eyes.

"You have no need to pretend any longer," Phillip stated firmly. "You have been caught attempting to take my painting from this house, using Lord Coates to take your guilt but it will not work, Lord Hemmingway. You must tell me the truth about what it is you have done. It is the only thing left to you."

Lord Hemmingway's jaw set as he looked back at Phillip,

though the spark in his eyes, Phillip considered, betrayed his fear.

"Lord Coates owed me a debt, as he has said." Lord Hemmingway shrugged but his voice was weak. "I wanted this painting and used him to get it for me."

"For what purpose?"

Lord Hemmingway looked away and did not immediately answer, appearing to struggle for a response. With a twist of his lips, he returned his gaze to Phillip. "It is worth something. I wanted it for financial gain. That is all."

"No, that is not all," Phillip answered, slamming one fist into the open palm of his other hand. "There is more, is there not? I have known from the moment I stepped into London that you despised me. You *and* Lord Pentland, though now I wonder if Lord Pentland is just a sycophant, doing as you instruct him to do whenever you wish it. Or mayhap he too owes you something, and you use that as leverage to have him do your bidding." Glaring at Lord Hemmingway and the insolent expression on his face, Phillip took another step closer. "Why do you hate me so? I have never done a single thing to either you or to any member of your family."

"Oh, but your father did *more* than enough!"

The voice of Lord Hemmingway flooded the room, and Phillip's chest tightened, seeing the color flood back into the gentleman's face.

"He was the very *worst* of gentlemen!" Lord Hemmingway exclaimed, coming away from the wall now and pointing one long finger in Phillip's direction. "Taking from others whatever he wanted, without even a *thought* about what is right!"

Anger shuddered through Phillip's frame. "And you

thought, in some way, to punish me for whatever wrongdoing my father acted against you?"

"Yes!" Lord Hemmingway threw up his hands. "I could do nothing! Your father had died, and the mourning period meant I could not come near. Why should I not do to you what he had done to me?"

"Because I am not responsible for my father's actions!" Phillip exclaimed, his anger still burning hot. "You attempted to force Lord Coates into this wicked scheme of yours, wanting *him* to take the blame for the very thing *you* had orchestrated! And all because of a grudge you have held against me because of my father?!" Hardly able to believe all that was being said, Phillip spun on his heel and marched back towards Lord Coates. "You told this man that he had to steal a painting from me, else you would… what would you do?"

"He said he would double my debt," Lord Coates said, heavily. "I could not bear the weight of even what I owed! To have it doubled would have been an impossible burden."

"You ought to be ashamed of yourself for your cruelty," Lord Fairchild said, his gaze trained on Lord Hemmingway. "To not only seek to punish Lord Coates for a debt he was, in time, to pay but to also take something of Lord Waverley's in an attempt to bring him even lower in his standing?" He scowled, eyes narrowed. "That is contemptible."

Lord Hemmingway said nothing, folding his arms over his chest and turning his head away from both Phillip and Lord Fairchild. Clearly, he had chosen not to say anything more.

"Lord Coates, might I ask you something?" Phillip asked as the gentleman looked back at him, his eyes shadowed. "Where did you put the painting when you took it that night? It has been hidden, has it not?"

Lord Coates' lips lifted in a mirthless smile. "As you know, I was acquainted with your father. He showed me, one evening, the passageway in this room. I assumed you knew of it but when I spoke with you, you did not mention it. I – I wanted to take it from the house that evening but the butler, the footmen, the maids and the other guests were all present."

"You were the one who pulled me from returning to the drawing room, then," Phillip said, speaking slowly. "Though was there a reason that I did not remember the evening at all? Did you... " Hesitating, he tried to speak as kindly as possible while, at the same time, determined to find the truth. "Did you give me something to make me forget?"

Closing his eyes tightly, Lord Coates trembled. One hand lifted, pointing to Lord Hemmingway. "He gave it to me," he rasped, not opening his eyes. "I tried and tried to find a reason that I could not do as he had asked, stating that someone would see me, that you would see me, and this... concoction of some sort was given to me." Opening his eyes, the gentleman looked straight into Phillip's eyes. "I did not want to, Waverley. I promise you. I wanted to fight against it with all of my being but Lord Hemmingway would not let me free."

"You had no choice," Phillip said, seeing the relief that smoothed some of the lines on the gentleman's forehead. "I can understand that. I do not hold you responsible, Lord Coates. It is solely Lord Hemmingway's doing." With this, he once more returned his gaze to Lord Hemmingway who, sullen, looked away.

"What will you do, my friend?" Lord Fairchild, who still had not moved away from the door, glanced at Lord Hemmingway and then back to Phillip. "Something must be done. The *ton* must know of this, at the very least!"

Phillip hesitated, a strange reluctance to pronounce judgment pulling hard at him. He knew his friend was right, Lord Hemmingway *had* done a good many things wrong and yes, the guilt was solely his but at the same time, Phillip had also to accept that his own father had been responsible for doing wrong to Lord Hemmingway.

"I will consider," he said, slowly, seeing Lord Coates rise to his feet. "At this present moment, I will not make a decision."

"Though, Lord Hemmingway, you must now consider Lord Coates' debt repaid in full." Lady Rosalyn spoke firmly, as Phillip nodded in agreement. "That was your promise to him, was it not? That if he stole this painting, then his debt would be forgotten. He has done so, and therefore, you have no more claim over him."

Lord Hemmingway started violently, his hands falling to his sides, his eyes narrowing, though whether it was from the unexpected way that Lady Rosalyn had spoken to him or the words she had said, Phillip could not be sure.

"If that is what you said to the man, then his debt is clear," Phillip agreed, coming to stand by Lord Coates. "Though if you wish to tell the *ton* what it is that Lord Hemmingway had you do, then I will not tell you to refrain, Lord Coates. What you do about Lord Hemmingway is entirely your own decision."

"I do not know how to thank you." Lord Coates turned and held out one hand for Phillip to shake, which he did without hesitation. "I did not think that this would be the outcome."

"You bear no guilt and none of my anger," Phillip assured him, seeing how Lady Rosalyn smiled gently at him. "Go now. Why do you not enjoy the rest of the play with your wife and daughter?"

Lord Coates smiled and, as he did so, the weight of all that had been discussed and all he had himself been carrying faded in an instant. "I shall," he said, his shoulders pulling back as he walked to the door, ignoring Lord Hemmingway entirely. Turning back to look at Phillip, the smile still lingering, he paused for a moment. "It is as clear to me as it has ever been that you are nothing like your father, Lord Waverley. Nothing like him in the least."

This sent such warmth of happiness through Phillip that he could not help the broad smile that spread right across his face. When the door closed, Phillip finally returned his attention to Lord Hemmingway, the smile now fading.

"Take your leave of my house and do not think for even a moment to ever darken my company again," he said, as Lord Fairchild opened the library door for Lord Hemmingway to take his leave. "And tell Lord Pentland I want none of his company either, though I may well speak to him myself and tell him just how poorly he has chosen his companions."

Lord Hemmingway did not need to be told twice. With a scowl still darkening his face, he practically ran from the room, leaving only Phillip, Lord Fairchild, and Lady Rosalyn.

"Goodness." Lady Rosalyn smiled but there was a sense of weariness about her as she came to join him, Lord Fairchild doing the same. "That was both terrifying and astonishing, though I am sure you are glad to have the painting back."

Looking at the cloth-covered painting that sat on the floor by the chair, Phillip considered, surprised at how little he had considered it. "I am glad to have found the truth," he said, slowly, "and relieved that Lord Coates had no guilt upon him in the end. As for the painting itself?" A wry smile pulled at his lips. "I care very little for that. I am not very well versed when it comes to artists and the like!"

Lady Rosalyn laughed as Lord Fairchild grinned back at him. "We are alike in that regard, then," she said, her arm slipping through his. "I am sure there is much more to consider, but for the moment, must you not return to your guests?"

The smile on his face turned into a grimace. "Yes, I suppose I must." It was the very last thing he wanted to do but given his slowly improving standing in society, Phillip knew he had no choice. "But will you both come to speak with me tomorrow? That will give me time to think on it all."

"Including what you will do with Lord Hemmingway," Lord Fairchild said, as Rosalyn nodded. "Yes, of course, we will call."

"Tomorrow, then," Phillip confirmed, making his way to the door with Lady Rosalyn on his arm. "Then all things, I hope, will be finally set right."

19

Rosalyn pushed open the library door, the nervous butterflies back in her stomach just as they had been the previous day. It was not because of Lord Coates' presence, however, nor because of the painting but simply because her brother had suddenly insisted that she go to speak with Lord Waverley at the proper time, whilst he lingered at home. He had said something about a business affair stealing all of his time from him but Rosalyn was quite certain there was something more to his intent.

This was, mayhap, the time for her to finish her conversation with Lord Waverley.

"Waverley?" She came inside, only to see him getting to his feet, a warm, welcoming smile on his face. "The butler said you were here."

"Where is your brother?" Looking over his shoulder, a slight confusion came into his smile. "I thought – "

"I think my brother wants us to speak in private," Rosalyn interrupted, albeit gently. "I could pretend that he is being held up by business affairs as he said to me but I know that is not the truth, as I am sure you do also." A heat rose in her cheeks as Lord Waverley's eyes rounded, only for him to chuckle, looking away and pushing one hand through his hair.

"Well, given the conversation I had with *him* recently, I suppose I should have expected this," he said, walking away from her before turning around. "Before we get to that, Rosalyn, might I ask if you are well?" His smile disappeared completely as he spoke. "Last evening, a good many things happened, and I want to make sure you are quite yourself."

Touched by his concern, Rosalyn smiled and put out her arms on either side. "As well as I have ever been, if not more so, given that this mystery has come to an end!"

"That is good." He tipped his head in the direction of the fireplace. "Lord Coates mentioned the passageway that my father showed him, though he did not tell me where it was nor how to open it." A light sparkled in his eyes, making Rosalyn's breath catch. "I asked my mother this morning, and she knew at once what I was talking about."

"Then you know where it is?"

With a nod, Lord Waverley stepped towards the fireplace, reaching for what appeared to be one of the books on the bookshelf. The book did not come out of its place, however, but stayed where it was, letting Lord Waverley pull it out towards himself, and the entire thing opened towards them. Rosalyn hurried forward, her eyes wide as she gazed down into the passageway.

"You did not know of this before? Truly?"

"I did not." Lord Waverley chuckled ruefully. "If I had, then it would have been the first place I might have looked for the painting!"

"Where does it lead?"

A touch of red came into his cheeks. "To my own rooms," he said, his eyes pulling away from her. "The rooms that were once my father's, which is mayhap why I never knew of the passageway."

A small sadness wound its way up through Rosalyn's heart and she came closer to him, her hand reaching out to take his. "Your character is vastly different from that of your father's," she assured him, his fingers closing around hers. "I see that in every way. There is nothing about you that is in any way displeasing."

"Nothing?" A twist of his lips told her that he did not agree with her. "There is much about my character that I find lacking."

"Oh?"

"My cowardice."

Rosalyn blinked, surprised. "Cowardice? I see none of that."

"I do," he confessed, reaching out to take her other hand. "Rosalyn, for years I have thought of you. *Years*, you understand? Ever since you made your come out some two years ago, my heart has filled with an ever-deepening affection for you… and I never said a word to you about all I felt."

This was something of a surprise to Rosalyn, who had not known before that he had felt such an affection for so long. She could only gaze up into his eyes, trying to understand, trying to make sense of why he had held himself back from her.

"I did not feel worthy of you," he said, as though he knew her question. "My father was bringing such shame to our family that I could not consider bringing you anywhere near to it! And then, thereafter, when I came to London, the sense of unworthiness pervaded nearly every thought."

"Oh, Waverley." Releasing his hand, Rosalyn reached up to press it gently against his cheek, aware of the thrill rushing up her spine as she touched his skin. "Did you truly believe that I, as a bluestocking, would care anything for what the *ton* might say?"

Closing his eyes briefly, he let out a slow breath. "I let myself believe things that were not true," he admitted, honestly, opening his eyes. "But then when you told me that you saw me as you saw your brother, any hint of hope died."

Wincing, Rosalyn set her hand on his shoulder. "I was deeply upset with you when I heard from your mother that you did not see me in the same way," she said, realizing now why he had said those things. "Now I realize why you could not admit to it."

"Because my feelings for you were nothing akin to what one has for a sibling," he answered, a broad smile spreading right across his face. "I think that my mother has known for some time of my feelings though she and I have never talked of it."

Rosalyn laughed softly. "Just as my brother has known of my heart before I even acknowledged the fact that I might have feelings of affection for you," she said, with a small sigh. "There were, on occasion, some things that Fairchild said that I did not fully understand. *Now*, I see what he meant."

Lord Waverley looked down at her tenderly, his free hand now settling about her waist as he pulled her ever so gently closer. "What did he mean, Rosalyn?"

The way her unfettered heart pulled her to him made her breath tumble in her chest, the promise lingering in his eyes begging her to speak.

"He meant that my heart has always been yours, Waverley," she answered, speaking carefully to convey all she felt. "I did not know it at first, I did not even see all that was so clear to others but now that I have recognized it, now that I understand it, it possesses me."

Lord Waverley's hand pressed hers as he looked down into her eyes, fervent hope now blossoming into joy. "My heart has never belonged to anyone other than you. I did not know what I was to do, truth be told, for to come to London and see you being pursued by other gentlemen was an agony I could not even begin to imagine!"

"But you shall never have to endure such a thing, I promise you," she said, moving closer now, closing the small distance between them. "Waverley, you see me and accept me as I am. You have never rejected me for being a blue-stocking, have never encouraged me to set it aside. Instead, you encourage me in it, delight in it, and even correct my brother in his attitude! How could I not love you? How could my heart ever belong to another?"

Lord Waverley began to lower his head but he did not kiss her, as she had expected. Instead, he wrapped both arms tightly around her and gazed deeply into her eyes, his breath warm across her cheek. "Rosalyn, you are unlike any other lady of my acquaintance. You are remarkable, truly remarkable, and it is an honor for me to call you my friend."

"Friend?" Rosalyn's eyebrows shot upwards and she pulled back from him a little. "Waverley, I thought – "

Laughing softly, he leaned close to her again, setting his forehead gently upon hers. "What I was going to say, my darling Rosalyn, was that I want to call you *more* than a friend. I want, with all of my heart, to call you my wife."

It was as if the world around her came to a stop, her heart forgetting to beat, her body forgetting to breathe. Her eyes affixed to his, the gentle smile on his lips, the hope lingering in his gaze assailing her heart. Tears came, unbidden, but as a smile broke upon her lips, they faded into the warmth that now infused her utterly.

"I love you, Waverley," she replied, her voice steady despite the way her heart sang with joy. "I love you with all of my heart and yes, I will marry you."

The crush of his lips to hers was unexpected but welcome, not slow and tender as she had thought but fervent and overwhelming. Her hands found his shoulders, then slipped around his neck as he pulled her tight against him, their embrace one of hope, of sweetness and love.

"I love you, Rosalyn," he whispered against her lips, barely an inch separating them as she clung to him tightly, her happiness complete. "Our future shall be one forged by love, binding us together."

With a soft smile on her lips, she closed her eyes and leaned into him again. "Together always, my love."

EPILOGUE

"My dear Rosalyn. How beautiful you look."

She smiled, feeling as though she were glowing with happiness. "Thank you, brother."

He came towards her, reaching to take her hands. "Are you ready for today?"

"*More* than ready."

Smiling at her as she stood in the vestry, ready to make her way into the church, Lord Fairchild took a long moment simply to look at her before he spoke again.

"Do you know something, Rosalyn? There has always been a faint hope, a vague thought, that such a thing as this might happen."

Her eyebrows lifted in surprise.

"For what could be better than for my sister to marry such an excellent gentleman as the Marquess of Waverley?" he continued, squeezing her hands gently. "He is one of my closest friends, someone I know who has the most excellent heart and whom I trust implicitly. I could think of no one better for you to marry, my dear."

Rosalyn's lips quirked. "You forgot one of the most important things, did you not?"

"Oh?" His eyes searched hers. "What is that?"

With a heart filled with love for Lord Waverley, Rosalyn let out a small, contented sigh. "He does not mind in the least that I am a bluestocking. Not only that but he encourages me in it, delights in how learned I am and wants to do all he can to aid me in my further study. *That* is one of the things that I have come to value about him, because he loves me for who I am rather than insisting that I change myself to suit what *he* requires." Aware there was a gentle rebuke in her words, Rosalyn smiled softly. "I want you to be happy also, my dear brother. I know that you have begun to care for Lady Catherine, have you not? Do you not hold a growing affection for her in your heart?"

Her brother frowned. "How do you know about that?"

Rosalyn laughed, hearing the organ music drifting towards her from the church itself. "Because you have danced with her three times, spoken about her almost every day since your first meeting, and because I have seen you lost in thought on many an occasion. Even through all of this, she has been an ever present consideration for you."

He shook his head, lips pursed. "I cannot think of her, not when her father – "

"Yes, you can." Rosalyn moved a little closer to her brother, gazing up into his eyes. "It was not *she* who had anything to do with the theft of the painting, was it?"

Lord Fairchild looked away, a touch of color on his cheeks. "No, it was not, but her family does not have as good a standing as I might have hoped. Besides which, now I know that her father is a little impoverished and that there is no hope of him bringing a decent dowry to the fore, so why... " Trailing off, he sighed heavily. "Why is it that I cannot stop thinking of her?"

Her heart leaped up at her brother's sudden vulnerability. "Because you have begun to care for her and I can assure you, no matter what difficulties stand before you, the affection you have in your heart will make them all very light indeed. Set your expectations aside and think only of what you have found growing in your heart. I can promise you, pursuing *that* will bring you a joyous, happy future. But to step away from what you feel will only bring you darkness."

After a few moments, Lord Fairchild began to nod and, as Rosalyn watched, a small smile touched the corners of his mouth.

"I think you are right, Rosalyn," he said, softly. "Seeing you as happy as this, seeing the way that Lord Waverley has lost his heart to you completely... well, I think I would like such a thing for myself also."

"Then you will pursue her?"

With only a second of hesitation, he nodded, a broad, warm smile spreading right across his face as if this decision had filled him with a new energy and fresh delight. "I will," he said, a little more loudly now. "Though let us make sure *you* are married first, shall we?"

Rosalyn laughed and took her brother's arm, her heart filled with anticipation at the thought of standing up and making her vows to Lord Waverley. "Yes, I think that is an excellent idea."

With another nod, Lord Fairchild took in a breath, glanced at her, and then nodded to the footmen to open the door. The music swelled and Rosalyn's heart with it, walking into the church but seeing no one but the Marquess. The softness about his smile, and the tenderness in his eyes made her heart lurch, her fingers tingling with the expectation of being able to reach out to take his arm though it was not yet time. She stood between her brother and Lord Waverley, still holding her brother's arm but looking towards her betrothed with nothing but love in her eyes.

"Dearly beloved," the clergyman began, the music now ended. "We are gathered together here in the sight of God, and in the face of this congregation, to join together this man and this woman in holy Matrimony; which is an honorable estate, instituted of God in the time of man's innocency, signifying to us the mystical union that is betwixt Christ and his Church; which holy estate Christ adorned and beautified with his presence, and first miracle that he wrought, in Cana of Galilee; and is commended of Saint Paul to be honorable among all men: and therefore is not by any to be enterprised, nor taken in hand, unadvisedly, lightly, or wantonly, to satisfy men's carnal lusts and appetites, like brute beasts that have no understanding; but reverently, discreetly, advisedly, soberly, and in the fear of God; duly considering the causes for which Matrimony was ordained. First, it was ordained for the procreation of children, to be brought up in the fear and nurture of the Lord, and to the praise of his holy Name. Secondly, it was ordained for a remedy against sin, and to avoid fornication; that such persons as have not the gift of continency might marry and keep themselves undefiled members of Christ's body. Thirdly, it was ordained for the mutual society, help, and comfort, that the one ought to have of the other, both in prosperity and adversity. Into which holy estate these two persons present come now to be joined."

To be joined. Rosalyn's smile spread wide as she closed her eyes for just a moment, taking in the significance of what lay before her. Their lives were to be joined together, each day shared with each other. Could there be anything more wonderful?

The clergyman cleared his throat, then gestured first to the Lord Waverley and then to her. "Therefore, if any man can show any just cause, why they may not lawfully be joined together, let him now speak, or else hereafter forever hold his peace." The clergyman paused for only a breath before continuing, looking down to them both. "I require and charge you both, as you will answer at the dreadful day of judgment when the secrets of all hearts shall be disclosed, that if either of you know any impediment, why you may not be lawfully joined together in matrimony, you do now confess it. For be you well assured, that so many as are coupled together otherwise than God's Word doth allow are not joined together by God; neither is their Matrimony lawful. At which day of marriage, if any man do allege and declare any impediment, why they may not be coupled together in matrimony, by God's Law, or the Laws of this Realm; and will be bound, and sufficient sureties with him, to the parties; or else put in a caution to prove his allegation: then the solemnization must be deferred, until such time as the truth be tried." Again, he paused for only a breath before smiling, clearly aware that there was nothing to impede them. "Then we come to the vows."

Rosalyn's heart began to quicken its pace, turning to look up at Lord Waverley, desperate now to put her hand to his arm, to have him close to her.

"Phillip, Marquess of Waverley, will you have this woman to thy wedded wife, to live together after God's ordinance in the holy estate of matrimony? Will you love her, comfort her, honor her, and keep her in sickness and in health; and, forsaking all other, keep only to her, so long as you both shall live?"

"I will."

Her heart swelled, happy tears in her eyes as the clergyman turned to her.

"Lady Rosalyn, will you have this man as your wedding husband, to live together after God's ordinance in the holy estate of matrimony? Will you obey him, and serve him, love, honor, and keep him in sickness and in health; and, forsaking all other, keep only to him, so long as you both shall live?"

"I will."

The clergyman smiled. "Then who gives this woman to be married to this man?"

"I do." With a press of her hand, her brother set Rosalyn's hand to the Marquess, and Rosalyn's breath hitched, the significance of the action not lost to her. Her fingers held tight to Lord Waverley's arm, hearing the clergyman offering him the vows he was to speak.

"I, Phillip, take you, Rosalyn, as my wedded wife; to have and to hold from this day forward, for better for worse, for richer for poorer, in sickness and in health, to love and to cherish, till death do us part, according to God's holy ordinance; and thereto I plight thee my troth."

The gentleness of his voice and the joy shining in his eyes as he looked down at her made Rosalyn blink furiously, fighting to keep back her tears of happiness. "I, Rosalyn, take you, Phillip, as my wedded husband, to have and to hold from this day forward, for better for worse, for richer for poorer, in sickness and in health, to love, cherish, and to obey, till death do us part, according to God's holy ordinance; and thereto I give thee my troth."

When the gold band was slipped onto her finger, Rosalyn could barely see it, such were the tears in her eyes. She was his now. The moment was upon them, the moment when she would be declared to be the Marquess' wife, and he, her husband.

As though he could sense her urgency, the clergyman lifted his hands to bless them. "I pronounce that they are Man and Wife together, In the Name of the Father, and of the Son, and the Holy Ghost. Amen."

"Amen," Rosalyn whispered, as she turned to face her husband. With one swift motion, the Marquess lifted her veil, and in that same instant, her tears receded. Finally, she was able to look up into his face, to see the love shining in his eyes. She had never felt such great happiness before, had never felt herself filled to the brim with light and joy.

"This way, my love," he murmured, leading her towards the small room where they were to sign their wedding lines. Rosalyn leaned into him, the door closing behind them, and though the clergyman moved forward, the Marquess kept her back.

"My darling Rosalyn." Lifting his hand, he ran his fingers lightly down her cheek, his eyes fastening to hers. "I cannot express to you the joy I feel in this moment."

"My heart feels it too," she answered, leaning into his touch. "In all the years we were known to each other, I did not think for even a moment that we would ever wed! And yet now, it is as though I have stepped into the light for the very first time as if those previous years were clothed in shadow even though I did not know it."

Lord Waverley smiled, then bent his head to kiss her; their first as husband and wife. Rosalyn pressed herself up on tiptoe, her arms going around his neck, his settling about her waist. They lingered for some minutes, lost in the embrace, lost in the love that they both shared, until reluctantly, the Marquess broke them apart.

"I suppose we should sign our wedding lines," he said,

with a smile. "Then I shall capture you in my arms again, my dear Rosalyn, and mayhap will never let you go."

"To be with you is the only place I want to be," she answered, her hand settling against his heart. "I love you, Waverley."

He took her hand and brought it to his lips, his eyes searching hers. "I love you too."

MY DEAR READER

Thank you for reading and supporting my books! I hope this story brought you some escape from the real world into the always captivating Regency world. A good story, especially one with a happy ending, just brightens your day and makes you feel good! If you enjoyed the book, would you leave a review on Amazon? Reviews are always appreciated.

Below is a complete list of all my books! Why not click and see if one of them can keep you entertained for a few hours?

The Duke's Daughters Series
The Duke's Daughters: A Sweet Regency Romance Boxset
A Rogue for a Lady
My Restless Earl
Rescued by an Earl
In the Arms of an Earl
The Reluctant Marquess (Prequel)

A Smithfield Market Regency Romance
The Smithfield Market Romances: A Sweet Regency Romance Boxset
The Rogue's Flower
Saved by the Scoundrel
Mending the Duke
The Baron's Malady

The Returned Lords of Grosvenor Square
The Returned Lords of Grosvenor Square: A Regency Romance Boxset
The Waiting Bride
The Long Return
The Duke's Saving Grace
A New Home for the Duke

The Spinsters Guild
The Spinsters Guild: A Sweet Regency Romance Boxset
A New Beginning
The Disgraced Bride
A Gentleman's Revenge
A Foolish Wager
A Lord Undone

Convenient Arrangements
Convenient Arrangements: A Regency Romance Collection
A Broken Betrothal
In Search of Love
Wed in Disgrace
Betrayal and Lies
A Past to Forget
Engaged to a Friend

Landon House
Landon House: A Regency Romance Boxset
Mistaken for a Rake
A Selfish Heart
A Love Unbroken
A Christmas Match
A Most Suitable Bride
An Expectation of Love

Second Chance Regency Romance
Second Chance Regency Romance Boxset
Loving the Scarred Soldier
Second Chance for Love
A Family of her Own
A Spinster No More

Soldiers and Sweethearts
Soldiers and Sweethearts Boxset
To Trust a Viscount
Whispers of the Heart
Dare to Love a Marquess
Healing the Earl
A Lady's Brave Heart

Ladies on their Own: Governesses and Companions
Ladies on their Own Boxset
More Than a Companion
The Hidden Governess
The Companion and the Earl
More than a Governess
Protected by the Companion

Lost Fortunes, Found Love
Lost Fortunes, Found Love Boxset
A Viscount's Stolen Fortune
For Richer, For Poorer
Her Heart's Choice
A Dreadful Secret
Their Forgotten Love
His Convenient Match

Only for Love

Only for Love : A Clean Regency Boxset
The Heart of a Gentleman
A Lord or a Liar
The Earl's Unspoken Love
The Viscount's Unlikely Ally
The Highwayman's Hidden Heart
Miss Millington's Unexpected Suitor

Waltzing with Wallflowers
Waltzing with Wallflowers: A Regency Romance Boxset
The Wallflower's Unseen Charm
The Wallflower's Midnight Waltz
Wallflower Whispers
The Ungainly Wallflower
The Determined Wallflower
The Wallflower's Secret (Revenge of the Wallflowers series)
The Wallflower's Choice

Regency Book Club
The Earl's Error

Whispers of the Ton
The Truth about the Earl
The Truth about the Rogue
The Truth about the Marquess
The Truth about the Viscount
The Truth about the Duke
The Truth about the Lady

Bluestocking Book Club
The Earl's Error

Christmas in London Series

The Uncatchable Earl
The Undesirable Duke

Christmas Kisses Series
Christmas Kisses Box Set
The Lady's Christmas Kiss
The Viscount's Christmas Queen
Her Christmas Duke

Christmas Stories
Love and Christmas Wishes: Three Regency Romance Novellas
A Family for Christmas
Mistletoe Magic: A Regency Romance
Heart, Homes & Holidays: A Sweet Romance Anthology

Happy Reading!
All my love,
Rose

A SNEAK PEEK OF THE EARL'S ERROR

PROLOGUE

"She takes far too much after you!"

Joceline winced as she sat in the window seat of the drawing room, hoping that neither of her parents became aware of her presence behind the curtain. She was doing as she always did at this time of the morning: reading in a quiet, cozy space with no one to interrupt her.

Though her mother and father believed that she was reading elsewhere and thus, they could speak openly and without her overhearing... though at this moment, Joceline very much wished that she could be elsewhere given that *she* was the topic of conversation.

"I know that you wish she was a good deal more like her sister, but I do not think there is anything wrong with Joceline's love of reading," she heard her father say, gently. "Come now, my dear, you are being a little too harsh, are you not?"

"Harsh?" The screech that came from her mother's lips had Joceline wincing, curling her knees up against her chest, her arms wrapping around them as she listened. "My dear husband, can you not see that we *must* find Joceline a match this Season? She has already had one Season and made little impact upon the *ton* in any way whatsoever! How are we meant to find her a suitable husband if she continues to behave in such a way?"

"In what way is she behaving?" Lord Melford asked, echoing Joceline's own sentiments. "Yes, she is quieter than Sarah was but that does not mean –"

"She knows too much and speaks of that knowledge without thinking!" Lady Melford interrupted, speaking loudly and over the top of her husband. "Yes, she is quieter but when she speaks, it is clear to all and sundry that she is nothing other than a bluestocking! You must prevent her from speaking out."

Joceline blinked quickly, a tightness growing in her chest though her pain was somewhat lessened by her father's hasty defense of her.

"I will not prevent Joceline from pursuing her love of reading, Martha," he said, with a firmness that had been absent from the conversation thus far. "I do not see it as a failing as you do. Rather, I think it perfectly suitable for any young lady to desire to expand their mind by reading and learning as Joceline does. It is a rare quality and one that ought to be supported."

There was a breath of silence and, in that moment, Joceline thought that her mother might step aside and agree to all that her husband had said... only for that idea to be knocked away.

"Supported?" she exclaimed, making Joceline's ears ring. "We cannot do such a thing as that! What will the *ton* say? What will society think? Believe me, if you do such a thing as this, then Joceline will never find a suitable husband."

"I do not think that is true," came the mild reply as tears came to Joceline's eyes, broken over how little her mother seemed to care for her and instead, cared only for the match that Joceline was one day to make. "There are bound to be other gentlemen in society with the same opinion as I."

This made Lady Melford snort disparagingly. "I hardly think so."

"Martha." This time, when Lord Melford spoke, it was with a trace of anger in his voice which, Joceline heard, seemed to quieten her mother a little. "I will not have you quash Joceline. I understand that you desire to see her wed and that is a good desire. I too have the very same. However, I will not permit you to force Joceline to hide that part of herself from the *ton*. It is not to be done."

"By why ever not?" came the question, a wheedling tone in the lady's voice now. "Why would you say such a thing? Can you not see that her chances of a successful match are much diminished?"

There came another moment of silence, only for Lord Melford to sigh heavily. "And can you not see, my dear, that her chances of a happy future are entirely extinguished if we force her to wed a gentleman who does not know who she truly is?"

Tears began to fall from Joceline's eyes, not only from the upset that came from hearing her mother speak so but also from the gentle comfort in her father's clear understanding and care of her. She pressed her hands to her cheeks, trying to stem the flow and doing her utmost to cry as silently as possible for fear of being discovered.

"I – I did not think..."

"We must consider Joceline herself," Lord Melford finished. "You may do as you please in London society, taking her to whatever occasions you think ought to be attended and presenting her to various gentlemen as you see fit. But do not ask her to keep her true self hidden from them all, for it will not bring her any sort of happiness though it might bring *you* a little contentment. Your desire to see all of our children married and settled is a good and reasonable one, my dear, but things are different when it comes to Joceline."

Lady Melford let out such a heavy sigh that Joceline could practically feel the frustration emanating from her.

"Would that she was more like her sister," Lady Melford muttered, darkly. "Sarah was everything a young lady of quality ought to be. You know as well as I that various gentlemen were pursuing her, though none are seeking out Joceline's company!"

"And our son made his own choice, and all has worked out well, yes I know." Lord Melford's tone sounded a little heavier now, as though he was tiring of the conversation. "Each of our children is very different to the others but that is not something to lament over, my dear. Please, we must think of Joceline's happiness over our own."

Another sigh and Joceline wiped at her eyes, the ache in her chest returning with a fierceness that stole her breath. Her mother complained a little more but Joceline barely gave it any attention, struggling with the awareness that she disappointed her mother a great deal.

It was not something that many young ladies were encouraged in, Joceline knew, for to be bluestocking was seen as something of an embarrassment, something that ought to be hidden away. Her father, the Viscount, had always encouraged her, however, both she *and* her sister to read and to learn and to explore as much as they wished, though Sarah had been less inclined to do so. Instead, she had dreamed of balls and dancing and courtship while Joceline had been learning about some far-flung countries whose people and practices were so very different from her own. Yes, Joceline had known that her mother was somewhat displeased with her learning and knowledge but she had never, until this moment, understood that her mother saw it as shameful. She believed that Joceline would never make a suitable match without pretending she was not as learned as she was and would be quite contented for her to marry a gentleman who did not know her as she truly was! Grateful for her father's determination and his continued encouragement, Joceline dried her tears and picked up her book again, the room now silent.

It is a good deal better than other young ladies, who have been told from the beginning whom they will marry, she thought to herself, her eyes flickering over the page as she fought to find her place. *I am still permitted to be just as I am in the hope that I can find a gentleman interested enough in me to overlook my bluestocking ways!*

A faint flickering hope that she would be able to do so quickly faded as she thought about her mother's concern and lack of belief that Joceline would be in any way successful. What would happen if, in her second Season, she had no more success than in the first? Would her father's attitude change? Would she be forced into a match she did not want?

Shaking her head as though to clear her thoughts, Joceline let out a slow breath and closed her eyes. She could not let herself think in such a way, not now, not when she had so much still to experience. At the present moment, she had her father's support and that *had* to be enough.

Besides, I shall have my friends around me, she thought to herself as the edges of her mouth lifted, bringing them to mind. *I shall not be the only bluestocking in London and mayhap that shall be enough to soften Mama's concern.* With that smile still lingering on her face, Joceline finally returned her full attention to her book and, with her mind now a good deal more settled, made her way into the story once more.

1

"Now, Joceline."

Joceline glanced at her mother as they stepped into the ballroom. "Yes, Mama?"

"This is not to be as things were last Season," her mother said, briskly. "You are to push yourself forward a little more. You are to seek to have your dance card practically *filled* at as many balls as we attend. You are to laugh and smile and converse – but not too much, you understand."

Fully comprehending what it was her mother was saying by making such a statement, Joceline nodded. "Yes, Mama." She had no intention of pretending that she was anything other than a bluestocking, however, for having overheard her mother and father's conversation, Joceline felt herself confident in her father's encouragement of her. "I shall do my best, certainly." This was meant in every seriousness though Lady Melford did not appear to take it as such, given the frown that quickly settled over her forehead.

"You are the only focus now, Joceline," she said, putting her hand on Joceline's arm as if to make sure that she was paying full attention. "I will be watching your every step and listening to your every word."

This made Joceline scowl.

"You may think that you can do as you please and continue as you did last Season but I am telling you now clearly, I will *not* permit it," Lady Melford stated, looking into Joceline's eyes. "You cannot hide behind your sister this Season and thus, you must be seen by others, known by others, and acknowledged by others. That is the only way."

Joceline nodded though, inwardly, her stomach twisted at the thought of trying to have a conversation with a gentleman that she did not know and who might not have any interest in knowing her! Sarah had been excellent in her conversation and her manner, able to have words flowing between herself and whomever she was speaking with, all within a matter of seconds, it seemed! Joceline, on the other hand, had found it difficult to speak easily with others, for, truth be told, the conversation had been vacuous and disinteresting. The talk of gossip had been most displeasing to her and she certainly had not had *any* thought of joining in and whispering about others in society! Even the imagining of it had been displeasing and thus, she had spent many a time in society standing very quietly indeed as her sister, mother or another in the group had spoken. She had been a very willing observer.

Not this Season, it seemed.

"Joceline!"

Her considerations flew out of her mind at a familiar voice and, turning, she quickly grasped the hands of Lady Rosalyn. "Rosalyn! How wonderful to see you!"

"And I you!" her friend exclaimed. "Goodness, it has been some months since we were last in company together and I confess that I have felt your absence every one of those days." She grinned, her eyes twinkling. "I have had no one to discuss the recent goings on in – oh!" Her smile cracked and she bobbed a quick curtsy, her gaze going over Joceline's shoulder. "Lady Melford, good evening."

"Good evening." Joceline's mother said, her tone a trifle cold. "Lady Rosalyn, I presume that you are not here alone?"

"Not at all, but I am being permitted to come and join my friend for a time," came the reply, as Lady Melford's lip curled just a fraction as though this was greatly displeasing. "I am grateful to know that I am trusted!"

Joceline, catching her friend's intention in saying such things, turned to look up at her mother. "Might I walk with Lady Rosalyn for a time? Just around the ballroom, no further."

Lady Melford drew herself up. "I am disinclined to permit such a thing, Lady Rosalyn. Joceline's dance card is not yet filled, though we have only just arrived."

This did not put Lady Rosalyn's enthusiasm to the test. "Then I shall return her to your side with every dance filled, I assure you. Good evening, Lady Melford."

With that, she took Joceline's arm and then hurried her away from her mother, pulling her to the quiet part of the ballroom so they might speak together.

"It is truly delightful to see you again," Lady Rosalyn said, squeezing Joceline's arm. "I was so hoping that you would be present, for there is much that I need to tell you!"

"Tell me?" Joceline asked, turning to look at her friend, a trifle wide eyed. "Is it that you are engaged?"

This made Lady Rosalyn laugh aloud, making Joceline's face heat. "No, no, not in the least. That is not something that I should undertake lightly. Since I have been away from London, I have not found any interest from any gentleman in the nearby vicinity of my father's estate. Though that is to be entirely expected given that they all only think of shooting and hunting and the like!"

Joceline laughed softly at this. "You mean that you have tried to engage them in conversation about other matters?"

"Indeed." Lady Rosalyn looked suddenly very serious. "I have tried to speak of the war and all that has been happening there but I am given nothing more than an incredulous look and then a stunned silence. Either they do not know what it is that I am speaking of or they do not think that a young lady such myself ought to know anything about it and thus, they do not wish to encourage me!"

With a grimace, Joceline sighed and looped her arm through her friends as they meandered slowly around the ballroom, forgetting all about her mother's expectation that she return with a full dance card. "That is not at all encouraging."

Lady Rosalyn nodded. "Indeed, it is not. My father is not particularly concerned as regards my unwed status, which is a relief, but then again, he is not particularly concerned about anything aside from his own estate and family name!"

Joceline smiled sympathetically. "That brings both its own difficulties and its blessings, I suppose."

"It does." Lady Rosalyn sighed and then, after a moment, gave herself a small, brisk shake. "But I do not mean to be throwing all of my concerns out on you. That is not what I meant when I said there was much I needed to tell you."

"No?" Joceline's interest quickened. "Then what it is?"

Lady Rosalyn beamed at her. "I have found some new friends and I have been *eagerly* awaiting your arrival so that I might introduce them to you." When Joceline nodded, Lady Rosalyn laughed softly. "You do not understand, they are not just any sort of acquaintances. They are all bluestockings!"

Joceline's eyes widened. "Truly?"

"Truly," Lady Rosalyn smiled. "Come with me now and I will introduce you to them all."

Allowing her friend to lead her, Joceline's eyes caught on a familiar face though there were two others that she did not recognize. "Miss Sherwood – Eugenia." She smiled and embraced her friend. "It has been so long since I have seen you!"

"Almost a year!" Miss Sherwood responded, as Lady Rosalyn smiled. "But we are back in company together again now, are we not?"

"And let me introduce you to two new acquaintances so that we shall be a merry little band of bluestockings!" Lady Rosalyn said, with a smile. "Lady Amelia, Lady Isobella, might I introduce you to Lady Joceline, daughter of Viscount Melford."

Joceline curtsied and then, as she rose, smiled warmly. "I am delighted to make your acquaintance, Lady Isobella, and yours also, Lady Amelia."

"And we you!" Lady Isobella exclaimed, her eyes alight with clear excitement. "Lady Rosalyn has told us so much about you and we have been eagerly awaiting your arrival here in London."

Joceline threw a sidelong glance toward her friend. "Just what have you been saying?"

Lady Rosalyn laughed. "I have been telling them that your father is supportive of your desire to learn and to read and the like. That is not something that all of us have been granted, unfortunately, though I know that we are *all* glad to have some solidarity."

"Indeed." Lady Amelia nodded fervently. "It is good to

know that there are other young ladies like us, those of us who seek to expand our knowledge and think it a good thing to do."

"Especially when society thinks it ill," Lady Isobella added, with a grimace as the light faded from her eyes. "It certainly does make one feel a good deal less isolated."

Joceline smiled at the small group, feeling her spirits a good deal lifted now. "You are right that I have my father's support but I certainly do not have my mother's and it is she who is here with me in London." Her smile began to dim. "I have overheard her speaking of my bluestocking ways with a good deal of disparity and that has made things a trifle difficult for me, I confess."

"I can imagine that must have been very troubling to hear also," Miss Sherwood said gently, her understanding and sympathy apparent in her expression and in her voice. "I am sorry for that."

Joceline hesitated, wondering if she ought to speak honestly when in the present company given that she had only just been introduced, but then she considered herself right to do so. "It was painful, yes. I confess to you all that my heart was sore upon hearing all that my mother thought of me but, at the same time, I was also grateful for my father's support and understanding. Though I do wish that he was in London with us!"

"He is not here?" Lady Rosalyn asked. "I thought he would be."

Joceline shook her head. "He was called away on business."

"I am here with my brother," Lady Rosalyn told her, with a wry smile. "So though he is just as disinclined towards my learning and the like, he is a little... distracted given the very many young ladies present and his own desire for a bride."

This made not only Lady Rosalyn laugh but the others with her and, as they did so, Joceline felt her heart squeeze with a sharp, fierce delight. She had not had any sort of camaraderie like this before! Yes, she had known Lady Rosalyn and Miss Sherwood the previous Season, but for there to be *five* of them who all felt the same way was quite different!

"I think we shall all be excellent friends," she said, making the other young ladies smile. "It will be an excellent Season, I am sure, now that I have you all with me. No amount of constant demands from my mother shall dampen my spirits, not now that I have friends with whom I can share my passion for reading." She chuckled softly to herself, a lightness in her spirit now. "In fact, even though I am expected to dance and to smile and to converse as my mother expects, I will have a fresh endurance, knowing that I have many a friend sympathizing with me as I endure dull conversations and the like."

Lady Rosalyn giggled. "Oh, we shall have to put up with many a frustrating conversation, I am sure! Do you know that the last time I tried to speak to a fellow about what I had been reading recently, he turned bodily away from me and showed me no further interest whatsoever?"

Lady Isobella gasped. "Goodness, that was most rude of him!"

"Indeed," Lady Rosalyn agreed, "though at least I knew that this was someone I am now able to ignore for the rest of the Season!"

This sent smiles around the small group and Joceline drew in a long, steady breath and then let it out again just as slowly. Here, she felt herself at ease – and that in the center of a London ballroom! She had never expected such a thing as this, had thought that it would be a good deal more difficult than this for her first ball and yet now, despite it all, she had not only met her friends from the past Season but also made two more acquaintances! Yes, she determined as she looked at each and every face, this would be a very good Season indeed.

Oh, it will be a very good Season! I am so glad this little band of bluestockings found each other. I hope they have the opportunity to solve a mystery as well as find love!

Check out the rest of the story in the Kindle Store: The Earl's Error

JOIN MY MAILING LIST

Sign up for my newsletter to stay up to date on new releases, contests, giveaways, freebies, and deals!

Free book with signup!

Monthly Facebook Giveaways! Books and Amazon gift cards! Join me on Facebook: https://www.facebook.com/ rosepearsonauthor

Website: www.RosePearsonAuthor.com

Follow me on Goodreads: Author Page

Printed in Dunstable, United Kingdom